Selected Stories

I. L. Peretz, 1892

Selected Stories

I. L. PERETZ

Edited with an Introduction by
Irving Howe and Eliezer Greenberg

SCHOCKEN BOOKS • NEW YORK

First SCHOCKEN PAPERBACK edition 1975

Acknowledgment is made to the publisher for permission to include "If Not Higher," "Bontsha the Silent," "*Ne'ilah* in Gehenna," and "Devotion Without End," from *A Treasury of Yiddish Stories*, edited by Irving Howe and Eliezer Greenberg, copyright © 1953, 1954 by The Viking Press, Inc.

Library of Congress Cataloging in Publication Data

Peretz, Isaac Loeb, 1852-1915.
  Selected Stories.

  Translated from Yiddish.
  CONTENTS: Berl the tailor.—The magician.—Thou
shalt not covet. [etc.]
PZ3.P4145Se [PJ5129.P4]   839'.09'33   73-91342

Contents

Introduction
by Irving Howe and Eliezer Greenberg

It is customary to speak of three figures—Mendele Mocher Sforim, Sholom Aleichem, and I. L. Peretz—as the founders of modern Yiddish literature, but for those readers who must encounter them mainly through the rough lens of English translation, they are by no means equally accessible or attractive. Mendele seems permanently locked into his culture, and while translators can give us approximations of his language, they cannot yield enough of his references, allusions, and satiric thrusts to enable an alien reader to understand why he is so highly regarded in the Yiddish world. Sholom Aleichem is a universal genius whose overflow of invention and humor survives *almost* any translation. But Peretz (1852–1915) presents us with a problem. His name is known and occasionally honored, his work is little read. More "modern" in outlook and sensibility than Mendele or Sholom Aleichem, he is nevertheless the most prominent among those Yiddish writers who turned back for their materials to the half-buried past of East European Jewish life. Deliberately cultivating the legends of the hasidic rabbis and retelling old stories that had been handed down in the Yiddish oral literature, Peretz submitted his restless mind to the enticements of a religious-folk tradition even as he was rejecting the formal systems of religious belief associated with it.

Let us be candid: except for the shrinking number of readers still at home with the culture of Yiddish, Peretz is not immediately available to the contemporary reader. At first glance—that frequent source of error—he may seem a writer of sentimental tales, folksy allegories, even obscurantist moralities. More than most writers, he can be retrieved for the literary imagination only by a return to his historical context.

I

I. L. Peretz was born in the Polish town of Zamosc, a lively and noisy place with a multilingual culture. Russian troops were stationed in the town, German merchants passed through frequently. While the Peretz family, apparently Sephardic in origin, was traditionally pious, the father, a prosperous merchant, had acquired some liberal ideas and was on the way to becoming a *maskil*, or enlightener. The young Peretz absorbed both the learning of traditional Judaism and the learning of modern Europe, the latter through lessons in German and Russian and an intense plunge into the secular library of a sympathetic *maskil*. "There were many-volumed novels," Peretz would write in his memoirs, "especially translations from the French of Dumas, Sue, Hugo, etc. I read them as they came into my hands, a volume 10 of Sue, followed by a volume 9 of Dumas, then a volume 3 of Hugo. . . . I devoured them just as they came." And while the Jewish community of Zamosc was fiercely opposed to the heresies of the Hasidim, the young Peretz sometimes would visit the *shtibl*, or little prayer house, of a local hasidic community, "attracted by their ecstasy . . . their warmth, their shouting, their beating on the wall during the silent prayer."

Orthodoxy dominated Jewish life at the time Peretz was growing up, but it was no longer an unchallenged Orthodoxy, it could no longer claim or hold completely the moral energies of a sensitive Jewish boy. By the 1870s a rasping struggle had begun between religious traditionalism and a range of new intellectual outlooks, some like the Haskalah, or Enlightenment, seeking to refresh Judaism through exposure to the winds of modern European thought, and others, like that of the socialist and some Zionist groups that would soon appear, frankly secularist in character and regarding Jewishness as no more than the culture of an oppressed group. In this struggle, which would persist for decades, Peretz stood at the very center, buffeted by the opposing tendencies and expressing opinions more ambivalent, certainly more complex, than could easily be grasped by ideologues on either side.

Peretz' early life—indeed, his life until middle age—is unimpressive. He seems to be drifting from one occupation, one interest to another, as if he does not know what his true purpose in life can be. An arranged marriage at eighteen which proves to be a disaster and ends in divorce; apprentice efforts at literary composition in Polish and, half-heartedly, in Yiddish; entry into the profession of law, successfully begun but not followed through; a second marriage in 1878, this time satisfying; some forays into Hebrew poetry; employment in 1890 as a sort of census-taker, really an informal sociologist, traveling from town to town and collecting information about *shtetl* life (this experience he recorded in an early book, *Bilder fun a Provintz-Rayze*, or *Pictures of a Provincial Journey*, 1891); finally a post with the Warsaw Jewish community, lasting the remainder of his life, which gave him time to write and, in effect, to become the central figure of Yiddish culture in Poland—all these are the motions and improvisations of a man trying to find his way, to discover what might stir him into an undeviating purpose.

There is similar drift intellectually. In the 1870s, as a young *maskil*, Peretz had looked down upon Yiddish as mere "jargon," a term of contempt employed by many Jewish intellectuals. After the pogroms of 1881, which set off the first great wave of migration to America, Peretz' feeling for Yiddish grew warmer and he began to yield himself to the cultural nationalism that was sweeping the East European Jewish intelligentsia, a movement romantic in voice yet intent upon a rationalist modernizing of Jewish thought. In the late 1890s Peretz went through a socialist phase, leading to his imprisonment for several months because he had attended an illegal meeting. A decade later he would be active in the Czernowitz Yiddish Conference, a gathering in Rumania at which distinguished intellectuals tried to accord status and dignity to the "jargon" which was in fact the vital language of millions of people. And at about the same time, though never joining the recently formed Zionist movement, Peretz expressed sympathy for the idea of a return to Palestine.

Eclectic and unsettled, he seems to have been open to almost any authentic impulse in Jewish life—except rabbinic orthodoxy. He was not primarily drawn to program or ideology as such. "He demanded of ideas," wrote his colleague Hersh Nomberg, "what one wants of a woman, that she be seductive, radiant, and amusing, yet not insist on a wedding canopy." What interested him most of all was a reassertion of Jewish intellectual energy, a regathering of Jewish morale. He was the kind of writer who must clarify his mind and achieve intellectual assurance before he can find his literary voice.

He had abandoned strict faith, yet it must be remembered
—this is perhaps the single overriding fact in the experience of
Yiddish writers at the end of the nineteenth century—that faith
abandoned could still be a far more imperious presence than new
creeds adopted. Like such Western writers as George Eliot and
Thomas Hardy, he found himself enabled to draw upon traditional faiths and feelings precisely *through* the act of denying
them intellectually; indeed, the greatest influence on the work of
such writers is the rich entanglement of images, symbols, language, and ceremonies associated with a discarded belief.

Peretz' earliest fiction in Yiddish inclines toward the satiric-
didactic sketch or, as in his *Pictures of a Provincial Journey* (see page
150), the social vignette, mordant in tone, somewhat realistic in
approach, but not finally devoted—he never would be—to de-
tailed social portraiture. At first Peretz published in Sholom
Aleichem's miscellany, *Di Yidishe Folks-biblyotek* (1888-89) but the
two writers, though warily respectful of one another, were tem-
peramentally at odds and held strongly varying notions of what
Yiddish literature should become. Besides, Sholom Aleichem
had taken too many editorial liberties with Peretz' long satiric-
reflective poem, "Monish," and Peretz had naturally resented
that. In 1891 Peretz issued his own collection, *Di Yidishe Biblyotek*,
which contained literary items and pieces of popular education,
and in 1894, *Yom Tov Bletlakh*, in which he published some of his
pungent essays calling for a cultural revival in East European
Jewish life.

What sort of a cultural revival? It is not always clear, since
Peretz had too restive and skeptical a mind to remain content
with fixed positions and was, in any case, far keener at criticism
than at making positive proposals. Criticism, however, was precisely what his culture needed: the scathing attacks he wrote on
the superficiality with which the newly secularized Yiddish culture took over bits and pieces of European culture, the insistence
he voiced that the course of modernizing could only be achieved
through indigenous means and materials. Better than anyone
else, Peretz saw that the burgeoning Yiddish culture, for all its
freshness and liveliness, was in danger of cutting itself off from
its historical roots in the Jewish past and that, in the long run, this
could only lead to a drying out and a withering away.

Peretz made his house at Ceglana 1 a Mecca for every aspiring
shtetl youth who fancied himself a Yiddish writer of the future.

One such youth, J. I. Trunk, later a distinguished writer, would remember the warm yet slightly sardonic reception which, as a *yeshivah-bokher* (yeshivah student) still dressed "in a long *kapote* [cloak] and traditional black serge cap," he was given by the now-famous writer wearing "a silk smoking jacket." Trunk brought along a high-flown story in Hebrew and Peretz offered a pungent criticism: "You think in Yiddish and translate yourself into Hebrew. . . . Why don't you write Yiddish? Doesn't it suit you . . . to write in the language of the common herd?"

Peretz was familiar with the thought of the West, at least those portions of it likely to reach the Warsaw intelligentsia at the turn of the century, and one strand of his creative self would always be cosmopolitan and skeptical. In his brilliant little essay, "Hope and Fear" he anticipated a central intellectual experience of our time, when he warned that the gods of secular progress might fail long before leading European writers would announce that their gods had indeed failed. Jacob Glatstein, himself a major Yiddish poet, has written that Peretz created "singlehanded a Jewish nineteenth century." By this striking phrase Glatstein means that Peretz succeeded in yoking together the worldly culture of Europe with the religious traditions of the Jews, or more precisely, that Peretz rediscovered and refined the Jewish tradition so that, on its own, it could slip into the era of intellectual modernism which begins in the mid-nineteenth century. To bring together the folk voice of the past with a vision of Jewish renaissance; to place, in Glatstein's words, "the inner nature of the Jewish spirit upon the world calendar of the nineteenth century" by unearthing "the finest Jewish treasures and illuminating them with the first electric light"—this was Peretz' achievement.

His work spread across several genres: the drama, the essay, the short story. Though his plays have been produced on the Yiddish stage, they are primarily reflective literary works: *Di Goldene Keyt* (*The Golden Chain*, 1909) focusing on a hasidic rabbi's determination to prolong the Sabbath into the seven days of the week so as to make all of life a sacred celebration, and *Baynakht oyfn Altn Mark* (*At Night in the Old Market*, 1907) creating a symbolic panorama of Jewish life in Poland that brings together the past and present, the living and the dead. Peretz' essays remain wonderfully fresh, full of intelligence and a certain impatience too, composed in a pithy and nervous Yiddish, hard to translate because free of those "literary" elaborations most translators like to indulge in. What Peretz did as an essayist was to mold for himself a distinctive form: brief, pungent, stripped to the essence of his matter, totally different from the slow-footed winding pace of earlier Yiddish writing.

But it is, of course, as a writer of short stories that he is best remembered. Like Hawthorne in America and Yeats and Synge in Ireland, Peretz cut a path to a literary future by falling back upon a native past. Among the Warsaw Jewish intellectuals, writes the Yiddish literary critic S. Niger in his definitive study of Peretz, there had developed during the 1880s and 1890s a strong interest in all forms of Yiddish folk creativity. The folklorist Judah Leib Cahan had begun to collect the texts and notations of old Yiddish folksongs. Other Yiddish writers were coming to recognize the diversity, richness, and even strangeness of the East European Jewish past as a source for their fiction.

This "national-romantic direction," as S. Niger calls it, prepared the way for Peretz' major work. At literary gatherings that took place on Saturday nights in Peretz' house, recalls Hersh Nomberg, "we used to sing folksongs. . . . In these songs of love and longing, joy and pain," the writers and intellectuals grouped around Peretz found support for their persuasion that the East European Jews, far from being "on one hand a Chosen People, elected, pure spirit and on the other, crippled, without feeling for nature, for simplicity, love, beauty, and poetry," were actually "natural, healthy human beings." Such persuasions are almost always likely to contain some exaggeration, insofar as they deny the spiritual and psychic costs of historical oppression; but it seems inevitable that they arise at the point when national minorities begin to assert themselves and press to reinforce their morale. The point that Peretz and his friends were trying to make about the experience of the East European Jews is not so very different from the point that writers like Ralph Ellison have in recent years been trying to make about the experience of American blacks: that even in the midst of oppression there has arisen a rich and various culture which cannot and should not be reduced to the terms of oppression.

In any case, this was a central persuasion behind Peretz' work, or perhaps more accurately, a dominating hope. Shortly before 1910 he published two volumes of stories—the major work of his career—called *Khasidish (Hasidic)* and *Folkstimmlikhe Ge-*

shikhten (Folk Tales) in which he embodied that persuasion or hope in works of the imagination.

II

Concerned with the reconstitution of the Jewish community at the moment it seemed to be turning from the Divine Presence to a secular European outlook, Peretz wished to find mundane equivalents for those values that the sacred tradition could no longer sustain. His vision of "the good Jew," as it emerges from his writings, is similar in tone and quality to the late nineteenth-century idea of "the good European." Peretz spoke for a Yiddish version of that liberal humanism and secular idealism which characterized the best minds of Europe at the end of the nineteenth century. In doing so, however, he sharply attacked all tendencies toward assimilationism among Jews, insisting that the Jews bring to world culture their own spirit, their own uniqueness, as an equal among equals. That restlessness, that fever, that coil of problems which we associate with the nineteenth century, Peretz brought into Yiddish life and literature. But he brought them, in the main, not through a diffusion of contemporary ideas, nor through his role—a role every Yiddish writer had to undertake—of popular educator. He brought the qualities of the nineteenth century into Yiddish literature by going backward into the East European Jewish past.

In his earlier and weaker stories Peretz faced both ways: outward, toward the themes and methods of European literature, and inward, toward the folk heritage. As he developed his distinctive style, he broke away from the methods of Mendele and Sholom Aleichem. Peretz writes with the plastic rapidity, the transparent nervousness characteristic of a great many modern authors. He brought, as Niger remarks, "impact and hurriedness into the structure of the Yiddish story: short-breathed, staccato, and aphoristic prose." The rhythm of Mendele and even Sholom Aleichem is the rhythm of a sleepy *shtetl*; the rhythm of Peretz, even when writing about hasidic rabbis and old Yiddish legends, is the rhythm of Jewish Warsaw.

In the earlier stories, often colored by feelings of social indignation over Jewish suffering and the decay of Jewish communal life (see "The Poor Boy," p. 144), Peretz comes closer to individual characterization than most of his Yiddish contemporaries. He focuses upon what might be called *typical individuals*, though not yet the fully individualized characters that nineteenth-century European literature sought to achieve. His people stand somewhere between the archetype and the fully formed individual: a hopeless youth, as in "The Mad Talmudist," torturing himself with his inadequacy, a pair of young lovers dreaming of happiness in a dismal Gorki-like cellar, as in "The Cellar."

In Peretz' later and stronger stories he reworks folk and hasidic materials in a way that appears to be folklike but is actually the product of a sophisticated literary intellect. The old properties, in their naïveté and charm, remain: Heaven is envisioned as a homely *beth din*, or rabbinical court, with an actual scale of justice, the legends contain "palaces" which testify to a poverty of imagination, or better, the imagination of poverty, and God Himself speaks out in anguish and impatience as if He were no more than a rabbi among rabbis. But together with the simple backgrounds and unadorned story lines, there is what Glatstein calls "an additional dimension of mind," with the "flavor of a modern story-teller added to their biblical clarity, so that they become neo-biblical moral fables." As he retells and deepens these stories, Peretz, the writer who measures the distance between himself and the pieties to which he turns back, is always though unobtrusively in sight, sometimes through his rearrangement of materials, sometimes through no more than an ironic phrase at the end of a story. His use of hasidic materials has been excellently described by Isaac Rosenfeld:

> The pragmatic stamp is on every word. The tone of wonder is given by the intelligence and not by the Hasidic awe it represents. Peretz shares the faith of which he writes but at a considerable remove, and it does not rest for him in the objects or efficacies of the Hasidic mystique, nor does it express a natural piety of utterance, as with prayer; his is a borrowed piety, taken from the intelligence, adept at translating one mode into another.

In the end Peretz must always part company with the hasidic wonder-workers and speakers of wisdom, for he cannot really share their oneness of vision, he can only offer variants and versions, completely honest in their approximation, which seek to break open the envelopes of doctrine in order to reach some fundamentals of wisdom. Accordingly, to quote Rosenfeld again, Peretz "took the Hasidic ecstacies not as ultimate things, visions in the midst of appearances . . . but rather as the immediate phenomena in the radiance of this world." Speaking from within the Yiddish milieu, S. Niger came to similar conclusions: Peretz had no desire to idealize the actual hasidic rabbis, "he sometimes made fun of them, having only a slight relationship to Hasidism in the narrow religious sense," and he consciously chose elements of the hasidic experience as "a medium for crystallizing his own thoughts and feelings." If, continues Niger, "Peretz in some sense became 'a Hasid,' it was only after having transformed Hasidism according to his own vision" (in Yiddish an untranslatable coinage, he *farperetzt* Hasidism).

There is a Peretz story, "If Not Higher" (p. 38), which provides a neat parable of his own literary situation. A skeptical Litvak, probably an oblique version of Peretz himself, expresses doubt over the goodness of the hasidic rabbi of Nemirov. He puts the rabbi to the test, secretly watching as the rabbi gets up early on a frosty morning, goes to the forest to chop wood, and then, disguised as a peasant, brings it to a poor widow whose cottage he warms and cheers with a lively fire. The inner anecdote about the rabbi Peretz took from a familiar hasidic story, told in many variations, about Rabbi Moses Leib of Sasov; but the encasing figure of the Litvak is Peretz' addition. After seeing the good deed performed by the rabbi, the Litvak becomes his disciple—a special kind of disciple, for when the ordinary followers of the rabbi say that their master ascends to heaven at the time of the Penetential Prayers, the Litvak adds quietly, "If not higher." The Litvak sees the saintliness of the hasidic rabbi as a *this-worldly* saintliness; he comes to adore the rabbi as a moral hero rather than as an agent of God. Peretz does not actually link himself to the world of the hasidic rabbi, he merely looks into it—with wonder and admiration, but still from a distance.

The most poised and complicated of Peretz' stories dealing with Hasidism is "Between Two Peaks" (p. 83) in which the phalanxed ranks of rationalism and enthusiasm, Orthodoxy and Hasidism, are aligned through two formidable protagonists; and at the end Peretz can only hope for a measure of patience, or tolerance, but not for a genuine reconciliation. In this story there is a recognition of irreconcilables, an awareness that some issues of mind cannot be dissolved by a mere shuffling of words. Yet, if the pointer wavers a trifle in any direction, it is toward the warmth and democratism of the hasidic view, as when the Bialer Rebbe says to his orthodox antagonist: "Teacher, tell me! What do you have for the people? For the simple craftsman? For a woodchopper or butcher? For the ordinary man? Most of all, for a man who is sinful? Teacher, what do you give to those who are not scholars?"

From Hasidism Peretz tried to extract its life-strength, but without finally crediting the source. Peretz found there, in Glatstein's words, "what Christianity often claims for itself: sympathy for the lowest classes, for the silent and abject—the spirit of Dostoevsky and Tolstoy. He did not need to read anything into Judaism, he read it *out*, from the depths of our moral existence." He wanted, in short, to discover in Hasidism unbreakable qualities of Jewish strength, and he did so with enough ironic self-awareness to recognize that even if his attempt was doomed to intellectual failure, precisely in that failure might lie its literary reward.

III

What kind of stories did Peretz write? It is not easy to answer this question, since, to our knowledge, there is nothing quite like his hasidic and folkloristic stories in Western literature. Perhaps the closest comparison—admittedly, not very close—is to be made with the stories of Hawthorne, also composed out of a quasi-allegorical intent, a heretical moral probing based on a lapsed religious orthodoxy, and some half-hidden, even sly touches of cleverness. Perhaps, too, there is a shade of comparison worth making with some of Kafka's shorter pieces. But in their essential qualities Peretz' stories seem to us unique: they have few points of similarity with the fictions we are likely to know in modern Western literature.

In its oral legends, anecdotes, miracle stories, and compressed moralities, the East European Jewish culture compressed, sometimes froze, its essential view of the world, its underlying spirit of distinctiveness. There are tales of the rare wisdom of rabbis, tales of rabbis bending from mere wisdom to a rarer goodness, tales of exemplary modesty, tales of outwitting enemies, tales of suffering and martyrdom; but also happier ones, tales of celebration, tales of purity, tales of the kindliness of the prophet Elijah as guardian of outcasts and the poor. These tales are completely imbedded in the culture, and scholars have had no difficulty in locating at least some of the sources and models for Peretz' work. Rarely do these tales go or seek to go beyond the limits of Jewish sensibility: they are at ease with their own assumptions, *as Peretz, in retelling them, is not.* Through the sociability of anecdote, a communion in which stories are exchanged as if they were gifts, the East European Jews maintained the continuity and coherence of their history.

Peretz took these rudimentary but sturdy anecdotes and retold them through a range of strategies. There is little physical description, little provisioning of the social scene, and little effort at the psychic delineation of characters. The physical world is taken for granted—what matters is moral discovery, spiritual action, the location of hidden weaknesses in the soul, the search for new sources of strength. A few figures reappear in a number of the stories: for instance, Berl the tailor, a characteristic East European Jew, rebellious in his younger years against God and accepting in his later, but hardly individualized or rendered with the depth of, say, Sholom Aleichem's Tevye. There is also Rabbi Levi-Yitzkhok, the most tender and humane of all the hasidic rabbis, advocate of mankind before the gates of heaven; but he too appears in his typicality, we neither know nor need to know more about him than is required by a single line of action. Finally, Peretz stakes all on the anecdote and its unravelling of implication.

Sometimes, when moved by the charm or pathos of the original anecdote, Peretz changes very little—as in the story "The Magician" (p. 25), which preserves almost intact the original folk sentiment of gratitude and awe at the arrival of the Prophet Elijah bringing help to the poor at Passover, or in "Devotion Without End" (p. 103), where modes of love are blended into a pure act of self-sacrifice. It would be a depressing kind of sophistication that disabled us from appreciating the inherent loveliness of such tales, even when they are not speckled by Peretz' irony. As he renders them, Peretz uses an utterly simple, unadorned, and transparent prose, so as to efface his own presence. At other times, as in the story "Three Gifts" (p. 41), Peretz allows the legendary material to unfold in its own right, and then, at the very end, there occurs a sentence crushing in its irony: after the three gifts of selfless martyrdom have been delivered to heaven, "the Eternal Voice declared: 'Truly beautiful gifts, unusually beautiful. . . . They have no practical value, no use at all, but as far as beauty is concerned—unusual.' " This concluding sentence can make the head reel; it comes as a shock of dissociation, perhaps despair, regarding the very purities of martyrdom Peretz has celebrated. At still other times, as in "The *Shabbes-Goy*" (p. 49), a sardonic assault on traditional rationales for Jewish passivity, Peretz puts a heavy imprint of his own sensibility on the story.

Almost always, however, Peretz' telling or retelling is notable for its tact, with the perspective of ironic complication clearly separable from the anecdote itself, and often demurely tucked away in no more than a turn of phrase at the end of the story. What we have, then, in these versions of traditional material, is the past recaptured, the past untampered with, the past radically altered and recreated, in an ascending line of difficulty and ambivalence; so that for all their thinness of narrative line and fragility of substance, the hasidic and folk tales yoke together Jewish past and Jewish present in a bond of tense affection.

In the main, the voice dominating these stories is ironic, ambivalent, skeptical, a modern voice that knows enough not to be content with being merely modern. The skepticism is sharpest in Peretz' single most famous story, "Bontsha the Silent" (p. 70), in which this archetypal *kleyne mentshele* (little, little man), whose life contained little of either good or evil,* evokes from the heavenly prosecutor "a bitter laugh," as if shamed before the paltriness of most human desire. Peretz—and here he does seem a little like Kafka—touches in this story on one of the major themes of modern literature: the radical, hopeless incommensurability between morality and existence, the sense of a deep injustice at the heart of the universe which even the heavens cannot remedy.

There are other stories, like the wonderful "The Hermit and the Bear" (p. 34) or "A Pinch of Snuff" (p. 58) or "Motl Prince" (p. 65), in which the thought is revealed through the tonality of Peretz' voice, that sharp *klugshaft,* or *khokhme,* Yiddish terms roughly invoking what we mean by cleverness and wisdom,

---

*Peretz, who knew something about Nietzsche, had an evident horror before the idea of moral vacuum.

which his readers would have immediately apprehended—and if not, so much the worse for them. Here the point of a story depends on a twist of dialectic, a seemingly casual turn of action or reflection: it is Peretz' mind in its relation with the Jewish tradition that provides the moral drama. In a story like "Joy Beyond Measure" (p. 78), where the Lord of the Universe trades the entire world to Satan in order to save the hasidic Rabbi Levi-Yitzkhok, we are left with troubling enigmas: Is this a trade of which Levi-Yitzkhok would have approved? What is the implied meaning that Peretz would bring to bear through the charm of the story?

In the hasidic and folklike stories we find, then, a whole range of perspective and tones, in their sum almost the totality of Jewish response to the Jewish situation. At their best, Peretz' stories ask to be read as "wisdom stories," pieces of fiction that evoke pleasure through a tacit engagement of mind, through oblique touches of cleverness, insight, commentary, through a sly negotiation of truth. What one hears, or overhears, in these stories is the Jewish mind at a certain point in its historical development, the Jewish mind engaged in self-reflection, self-argument, self-criticism, but most of all, self-discovery. The "wisdom story" is a fiction in which the pleasure resides not merely, perhaps not even mostly, in the matter itself, but rather in the conduit of argument that is established between the mind of the writer and the mind of the reader as both reflect—with the typical Jewish gesture of two fingers of one hand striking the palm of the other—on what the story can yield. It is a kind of fiction, to twist Robert Frost's remark about poetry, that begins in delight and ends in wisdom.

Berl the Tailor

It is the eve of Yom Kippur at the Berdichev synagogue. Night falls. The old people have finished their prayers. Rabbi Levi-Yitzkhok* stands before the lectern. The time has come for him to chant the Kol Nidre—but he remains silent.

All eyes rest upon his back. In the woman's section there's a stillness as before a storm. Perhaps, as is his custom, Levi-Yitzkhok will begin with a few words of his own, talking things over with the Almighty, as a man talks to a friend: in Yiddish.

But Levi-Yitzkhok remains silent, wrapped in his *kittl*, a linen prayer-robe, and his *tallith*, a prayer shawl.

What does this mean?

Have the gates of prayer been shut? Does he lack the strength to knock upon them? He stands there, somewhat bent, one ear cocked, as if listening to something up above. Is he trying to hear whether the gates will open?

Suddenly Levi-Yitzkhok turns toward the congregation and calls to the sexton—"*Shammes!*"

The *shammes* hurries over. Levi-Yitzkhok asks him, "Berl the tailor, is he here yet?"

The congregation buzzes with astonishment. The *shammes* doesn't know, he stammers, starts looking around. Levi-Yitzkhok also looks.

"No," says Levi-Yitzkhok, "Berl isn't here, he's stayed home." And he turns once more to the *shammes*: "Go to the house of Berl the tailor and tell him to come here! Say that it is I, Rabbi Levi-Yitzkhok, who calls him."

So the *shammes* goes.

---

*Levi-Yitzkhok is the name of an actual figure in East European Jewish life, one of the hasidic masters of the late eighteenth century (Levi Isaac ben Meir of Berdichev, c. 1740-1810). He was noted for his humaneness, good nature, and kindliness.

Berl the tailor lives in the synagogue alley. It takes only a minute to get there. He comes, Berl the tailor, without his *kittl* and without his *tallith*, dressed in his workday clothes, with a tense look on his face, half-angry, half-frightened. He goes up to Levi-Yitzkhok: "You sent for me, Rabbi, so I came to you." He stresses the "you."

Levi-Yitzkhok smiles. "Tell me," he says, "Berele, why are they talking about you so much up there? The heavenly circles are full of you. You've created such a commotion! All they do up there is talk about Berl the tailor, Berl the tailor."

"Aha," exclaims Berl with a grimace of satisfaction.

"You have a complaint, perhaps?"

"Of course."

"To whom?"

"The Almighty!"

The congregation grows restless, it would like to tear this little tailor from limb to limb, but Rabbi Levi-Yitzkhok only smiles more broadly: "Perhaps you'll tell us, Berl, what it's all about?"

"Why not?" answers Berl. "Certainly. I'm even ready to summon a rabbinical court to hear my case."

"Speak."

And Berl the tailor speaks: "All summer long there wasn't a stitch of work, not from Jews, not from peasants. You might as well lie down and die."

"It's hard to believe," says the rabbi. "Abraham, Isaac, and Jacob are merciful fathers, you should have confided in them."

"No, not about this, Rabbi. I don't ask and I don't take. . . ."

Berl accepts charity from no man, he has as much of a share in the Almighty as anyone else. What he did was to send his daughter to work as a servant in a larger town.

And he, Berl, sits at home, waiting to see what His Beloved Name will bring.

It is just before Sukkoth. The door opens. Aha!, he thinks. And there enters a messenger from the nobleman of the district. They want him to reline a coat.

Good! The Almighty provides sustenance. So Berl sets out and comes to the nobleman's palace. He is taken to a chamber, where they give him wool and fur pelts.

"You should have seen those pelts, Rabbi, beautiful fur of foxes."

It's time for Kol Nidre, the rabbi reminds him. "All right, you relined the coat, you did a good job. What happened next?"

"A trifle . . . three pelts remained."

"You took them?"

"It's not as easy as it sounds, Rabbi. When you leave the palace, there's a guard at the gate. If he wants, he searches you, right down to your boots. And if he finds those pelts on you, they have dogs and they have whips."

"So what did you do?"

"It's not for nothing that Berl is Berl. I go into the kitchen and ask them to let me take home a loaf of bread. Not, heaven forbid, for eating. They give me the bread, I take it back, cut it open, hollow it out, knead the soft insides until it's all soaked with sweat. Then I throw it to the dog that's lying at the gate. Dogs, you know, like human sweat. And meanwhile I stuff the three pelts into the empty loaf.

"And I'm off!

"At the gate of the palace a guard cries: What are you carrying there, Jew boy, under your arm?'

"I show him: a bread.

"I get past him safely and start making tracks. I keep away from the road and cut across this field, across that field—it's quicker.

"I hurry along and every once in a while break into a little jig: it will get me a citron, a palm branch. Not the community's, not borrowed, but my own. . . . Darling little pelts.

"Suddenly the earth starts trembling under me. I hear a sound. A guard is chasing me, I'm scared to death. They must have counted the pelts. . . . It's foolish to keep running, the guard rides the nobleman's horse. . . . So I throw the bread into the bushes, make a clear mark at the spot, and wait. They call me: 'Berke, hey, Berke!'

"It's the nobleman's little Cossack, I know his voice. I can't stop trembling, Rabbi, I tremble and tremble. My soul drops to my boots, but still, I'm Berl the tailor, so I turn around and go up to the Cossack as if nothing is wrong.

"It turns out to be a needless fright.

"I forgot to sew a hook onto the coat, so they sent the guard after me. He helps me onto his horse, and we're off.

"I sew on the hook, thank my stars, and go back.

"But when I reach the place that I've marked—it's not there. No bread!

"It's long past harvest time, no one is in the fields. Not a creature has passed by, no bird could lift up such a load. So I soon figure out who is at the bottom of all this."

"Who?" asks Levi-Yitzkhok.

"He," answers Berl the tailor, pointing to the sky. "The Almighty! It's the work of His hands. And I know why, too. The Master of the Universe doesn't want His servant, Berl the tailor, to steal. . . ."

"Of course," murmurs Levi-Yitzkhok, "it's the law. . . ."

"The law, shmaw!" shouts Berl. "Surely He knows that a custom comes before a law. And it wasn't I who invented this age-old custom.

"But then again," argues Berl, "let's look at it from another side. If the Almighty is such a great and proud lord, and doesn't want even His poorest servant of servants, Berl the tailor, to steal—then let Him provide livelihood! Let Him give us a piece of bread, the way a lord should. But He neither gives bread nor permits us to take it. And therefore," concludes Berl, "I no longer want to serve Him. I have made a vow—an end to it!"

The congregation starts to growl. Hands are lifted. They grow more and more restless. But Levi-Yitzkhok orders: "Quiet!"

He turns to Berl, and in a gentle voice: "Well, and what else?"

"Nothing else! I come home, I don't wash, I eat without saying the blessing. My wife dares open her mouth—I smack her one! I go to bed without prayers. My lips want to recite the words automatically, but I grit my teeth. In the morning—no blessing, no washing of hands, no prayers. 'Bring the food!' I shout. My wife runs away, back to her father. So who needs a wife! I get some satisfaction out of that, at least. I'm Berl the tailor, but she is just a weak woman. Who needs her mixed up in all this? And I do what I have to do: no *sukkah*, no citron, no palms. . . . Sometimes I take myself a drink, but no Kiddush on the holidays. No; on Simhath Torah I grab a sack and like Mordecai after the verdict I pull it over my head. Out of spite, sheer spite!

"Comes the Days of Penance, it gets a little depressing. The *shammes* knocks, my heart knocks. It draws me. . . . But no, I'm Berl the tailor! A man of his word! I close my ears and bear it. Comes Rosh Hashanah—I don't budge. The time comes for blowing the *shofar*, I stuff my ears with cotton. My heart yearns, it tugs at me. . . . I am sick of myself, I go unwashed, unclean. There's a bit of mirror, I turn it around to the wall. I don't want to see my ugly mug. I hear people going to *Tashlikh*, the casting out of sins at the river, but. . . ."

He stands there for a while, then cries out: "But I'm right, Rabbi! I won't be put off with just anything."

Levi-Yitzkhok meditates a little. "And what do you do, Berl? Livelihood?"

Berl is offended. "The devil with livelihood! Livelihood He should have given earlier. Livelihood is due to everyone, even the bird in the air, the worm in the ground. No, Berl the tailor wants something more than that!"

"What is it, Berl, tell us——"

And Berl speaks out: "Isn't it true that Yom Kippur atones only for the sins between man and God?"

"It's true."

"But not for the sins between man and man?"

"No!"

Berl draws himself erect, taut as a string, and in a high, strong voice, says: "Then Berl will not submit to Him. I will not serve the Lord again until He agrees, this year, to forgive the sins of man against man."

"Am I right, Rabbi?"

"Right!" says Levi-Yitzkhok. "And if you stand fast, they will have to give in to you."

Levi-Yitzkhok turns back to the Ark, looks up, listens for a few minutes, and then reports: "You have prevailed, Berl! Go home—go and get your *kittl* and your *tallith!*"

Translated by Irving Howe and Eliezer Greenberg

The Magician

A magician once came to a village in Volhynia.

It happened in that busy time before the Passover season, when a Jew has more problems than hair upon his head. Nonetheless, he created a sensation. A mysterious man! In tatters—yet he had a stovepipe, even if wrinkled, on his head. His face was obviously Jewish: the revealing sign was somewhere on his nose. As opposed to this, his beard was shaven. He had no passport. Moreover, you never saw him eat—kosher food or no. How could one tell what sort of man he was?

You asked, "Where from?" He answered, "Paris." "Where to?" "London." "Why did you come here?" "Lost my way." He must have walked. And he doesn't go to the synagogue for prayers. Not even on Saturday before Passover. If people get too close, if a circle forms around him, he suddenly disappears, as if into the earth—until he re-emerges on the other side of the marketplace.

Meanwhile, having rented a hall, he started to perform.

Amazing! In front of the whole community he swallowed live coals as if they were noodles. He drew all kinds of ribbons from his mouth: red, green, any color you wanted—each as long as the Exile. From a bootleg, he pulled sixteen pair of turkeys, the size of bears and lively—prancing around the stage. Then he lifts a foot and scratches off the sole a basinful of golden coins. After the applause, he whistles. White loaves of Sabbath-bread flock like birds into the air and begin to do a wedding-dance beneath the ceiling. A second whistle and, in the wink of an eye, they vanish. As if they never were. No white breads, no ribbons, no turkeys! Nothing!

We know the Adversary also has powers. The sorcerers of Egypt probably were able to perform tricks even more remarkable. But still, it is a puzzle! Why is he such a pauper? He peels golden ducats off the bottom of his shoe but hasn't got enough for his room at the inn. With a single note, he bakes more loaves than our biggest baker. He knows how to pull turkeys out of his boot top. But his face is drawn, hunger burns in his eyes. Many who look stronger have already been buried. Jokers say that this is the fifth question of the Passover seder.

Before we reach the seder, let us leave the magician and turn to Hayim Yoine and his wife Rivke Beyle. He had once been a dealer in timber. He had bought a forest at a reasonable price. Then the area was closed to further cutting. He was left with nothing but a single shirt! Hayim Yoine became a clerk for another man in that business: then he lost this job and, for several months, has been earning nothing. They have survived the winter—but in what a fashion! (The same to all anti-Semites!)

After winter, come the new demands of the Passover season. All they once had has already been pawned, from the hanging candlestick to the last pillow. Rivke Beyle tells him, "Go to the community and take the money they give you to buy flour for matzohs." Hayim Yoine says he is sure the Lord will help them: there is no reason to lose face. So Rivke Beyle looks once more in every corner and, this time, she finds a worn old silver spoon. A miracle from heaven! Really! It is ages since the spoon had been mislaid. Hayim Yoine took it and, when he sold it, contributed the pennies to the community fund for flour to make matzohs, saying the poor had more need for money than he did.

Time passed. A few weeks to Passover. He remains confident. God does not desert you! Rivke Beyle is silent. A woman must obey her husband. A day goes by—another follows. Rivke Beyle is incapable of sleep. Her face burrowing into the straw mattress, she weeps silently, so he should not hear. There is no sign of their getting anything for the Seder. Days are worse than nights. At night a woman is able to weep her heart out. But in the daytime you have to pinch your cheeks to keep a little of the color. Some of the neighbors stare; they keep studying her face and their pitying looks stab like needles. Others want to probe, "When are you baking matzohs? Where are you with your beets?" Those who know her better say, "Is something wrong? Rivke Beyle, what is the matter? If you need anything, we'll lend it to you, and so forth. . . ."

Hayim Yoine won't accept a present from a mortal being and, since Rivke Beyle will not go against her husband's wishes, she keeps coming up with new explanations and excuses—but her face is flushed.

The neighbors, seeing something is not as it should be, hurry to the rabbi. The rabbi listens sadly; he sighs and ponders. Finally he answers that Hayim Yoine is a pious and a learned man. If *he* is confident, that is the way we must leave it.

Rivke Beyle doesn't even have candles for the Benediction. And here it is Passover already!

Hayim Yoine walks home from the synagogue. He sees all the windows in the market square shining with a festive joy. Only his are desolate. Like a mourner among wedding guests, a blind man among the seeing.

But he was not discouraged. "If God desires, there will still be a proper Seder." He walked into the house with a "Happy holiday!" Again—cheerily—"A happy holiday to you, Rivke Beyle!" And her tear-filled voice came from a gloomy corner. "Happy holiday! Good year!"

Her eyes were like burning coals. So he went over, saying, "Rivke Beyle, this is a time for joy. Don't you understand? The Exodus from Egypt. Mourning is forbidden. And besides—what is there to mourn? If God doesn't want us to have our own Seder, we must willingly accept it and go to another's. That is what we'll do. We'll be welcome anywhere. All the doors are open. At this very moment, people are reciting, 'Let all who are hungry come into our house. . . .' Put on your shawl. We'll go to the table of some decent man."

Rivke Beyle, who always listened to her husband, held back the cry that was bursting from her throat. She took her ragged shawl and was about to leave. But at that moment, the door opened and someone entered, saying, "Happy holiday!"

"Happy year!" they answered, though they were not able to make out who this person was.

Said the one who entered, "I would like to be a guest at your Seder." So Hayim Yoine replied, "We do not even have a Seder for ourselves." And the other said he brought the Seder with him.

"In the dark?" Rivke Beyle was unable to control her sobs.

"Not at all," he answered. "We are going to have light." And he made a pass—"Hocus-pocus"—and two silver candlesticks, with burning tallow candles, appeared in the air. The room lit up. Hayim Yoine and Rivke Beyle saw that it was the magician. They gaped and, in terror and surprise, were not able to speak a single word. Holding each other's hands, they stood with their eyes and mouth wide open.

The magician turned to the table that stood demurely in the corner. "Now, youngster! Cover up and come here!" As soon as he said these words, a snow-white cloth dropped down from the ceiling and covered the table—which began to move till it reached the middle of the room, where it came to rest precisely under the lights. And then the silver candlesticks lowered themselves and rested on the cloth.

"Now," said the magician, "all that we need is couches for reclining. Let us have couches!" Whereupon, three benches —from three corners of the room—moved over to the table and positioned themselves along three of its sides. He told them to be wider. They became wider, turning into armchairs. He said, "Softer!" They got covered with velvet. Then, at his order, snow-white pillows fell from the ceiling and, at his command, settled upon the armchairs and, lo, they were three couches. Also at his words, there appeared a platter with the required items and set itself on the table-spread. Also—red wine cups, wine flasks, and matzohs. Even Haggadahs with gilt edges to the pages.

"Have you water for washing?" the magician asked. "I can bring that too."

It was only then that they woke from their amazement. Rivke Beyle whispered in Hayim Yoine's ear. "Is all of this permitted?" He didn't know. So she gave him counsel. "Go and ask the rabbi." But he answered that he couldn't leave her alone with the magician. He told her to go there. She said, no, she is just a foolish woman. The rabbi won't believe her. He will think she's lost her senses. So they finally went to the rabbi together and they left the magician at the Seder.

The rabbi said, what is made by sorcery has no tangible existence. It is merely a delusion. He told them to go home. If the matzah will let itself be broken, the wine to be poured into the goblets; if the pillows can be touched—that would be proof that all is proper, sent from Heaven and to be enjoyed.

That was the rabbi's judgment. Hearts beating, they went back. They walked into the house. The magician was gone. But the feast was there—as it was before. A pillow can be patted. The wine can be poured. The matzohs can be broken. . . . Only then did they realize that this was the Prophet Elijah. And they had a happy holiday.

Translated by Nathan Halper

Thou Shalt Not Covet

As you all know, every Jew must fulfill all the commandments of the Torah. And whatever one fails to perform in one incarnation, must be made up in another. The faults of one incarnation have to be made good in another because the soul must return to the throne of glory perfect and without fault, pure and without blemish. Those who perform all the commandments of the Torah are therefore elevated before their time, without the agonies of death and without the torments of the grave. Great saints undergo but one incarnation, or at most two, while ordinary mortals—may you be spared such a fate!—undergo a hundred or more incarnations. Nor is it rare for a person to pass from one incarnation to another till the end of all generations, when death devours him forever and his soiled soul will be judged in the Vale of Jehoshaphat or the Valley of Jezreel.

But this is not what I want to talk about now. What I want to tell you is how through some trivial matter, a mere nothing, one may be doomed to an extra incarnation, and, as is customary, once one starts to fall, one falls ever lower and lower.

It came to pass that a great saint was about to complete his cycle of incarnations in this world. His soul was about to fly up to its home, to the throne of glory from which it had been hewed, pure as gold, pure as purity itself. Up above there was commotion and a rush to the gates of heaven to welcome the pure soul—but at the last moment the joy was disturbed.

In his last incarnation this saint had been noted for his contentment; he was satisfied with little; he was a man who had not tasted the pleasures of this world—he observed fasts and devoted himself to study. All his days he had been a man apart from the vanities of life. When his time came to leave this world, he experienced—may you be saved from such an ordeal!—very difficult death throes. His body refused to part from his soul and be consigned to a dark grave. His body argued: I have not lived yet, I have not yet enjoyed my share of life. Every limb resisted the Angel of Death. The heart said: I haven't felt anything yet. The eyes protested: We haven't seen anything yet. The hands: What have we ever held? The legs: Where did we ever go? And so also with all the other parts. The angel who had been sent to fetch the saint's soul had to battle every limb, every vein, every drop of blood, for all of them held on to the soul as if with pincers, and the angel had to extract the soul as one picks a delicate rose from among sharp thorns. The death agonies were therefore so great, and the pain of separating the soul from the body so excruciating, that at the last moment, well after he had recited the confession and with his last breath, the saint gave way for an instant and sighed. The sigh was a sigh of envy—he envied those who enjoyed an easy release from life, he wished for an easy death. Yet no time was left to repent this envy. And because he transgressed against the commandment not to covet—for a Jew must not covet even an easy death—the preparations for his welcome on high were halted and the gates of heaven locked again. This saint had once more to be reincarnated in order to correct the fault of being covetous.

Still, there was much pity for this saint in the upper worlds and some of the heavenly host were even displeased with the Angel of Death for not having halted a moment so as to give the saint an opportunity to repent. It was decided that, at the least, the saint's trial should be eased, that in his coming incarnation he should enjoy a blessed and lucky life so that he should have no cause to envy anyone, no reason to covet anything—and he was also assured of an easy death.

Satan heard this and smiled. Not so fast. He won't let him out of his hands that easy.

And so this saint was reincarnated. This time in the guise of Reb Zeynvele Purisover.

Who is Reb Zeynvele Purisover?

A man—may all Jews be like him! A lord. He lacked nothing. As a scholar he excelled the rabbi himself. As a singer, he was better than the cantor. When it came to reading the Torah, he was much better than the teacher, that Litvak. And his wife—work burned under her hands. And his children—the finest. And a livelihood right at home. And on top of all this he had the finest house in town, and gave most generously to charity. Right inside the house he had the finest *sukkah* in town bedecked with fruit from the Holy Land. Who owned the finest ethrog resting in the most expensive silver container? Reb Zeynvele. Who was the most honest arbitrator and wisest counselor? Reb Zeynvele. Should he perhaps covet the post of *gabbai*, or deacon, in the synagogue, when all the *gabbaim* do not lift a finger without first consulting him? Not even the *shammes* dares stir without getting the nod from him.

Reb Zeynvele devoted himself to study and good deeds, his eyes shine beneath his high forehead like those of an ancient sage. He opens his mouth—pearls, not words, come pouring out. And a handsome man he is too, a genuine king. His white beard is curly, his *shtrayml* rimmed with silvery fur, his satin caftan held together with silver hooks. In a word—learning and greatness rolled in one.

You might suppose, then, that this would be his last incarnation. No, it might have been so, if it weren't for the unmentionable one.

One day he—Satan, that is—appears in the guise of a wayfarer. An ordinary young man from somewhere, hunchbacked, altogether unprepossessing. He comes on a winter evening into the synagogue around the time of the evening prayers and sits down by the oven. Naturally, Reb Zeynvele invites him home for dinner, he is always on the lookout for dinner guests. The hunchback follows him home. Between one course and another they discuss learned matters, naturally. A son or a son-in-law of Reb Zeynvele starts off with a difficult problem and all eyes turn to Reb Zeynvele. He will handle the matter. Reb Zeynvele smiles and meanwhile honors the guest by asking him to say grace. The guest finishes and Reb Zeynvele begins to speak. What he says is so clear, so obvious, that it seems he is laying down a straight, broad, snow-covered highway, white and spacious and smooth as the top of a table—get into a sleigh and off you go. The sons and sons-in-law are all ears and glow with the pleasure of it all. The hunchback looks sideways disapprovingly and smiles with his thin lips. Reb Zeynvele notices this and asks, "You don't agree?"

The hunchback answers insolently, "Not in the least."

Reb Zeynvele asks, "Why?"

And he, the hunchback, begins to explain why, and a debate ensues.

The hunchback skips through the entire Talmud and its summaries; he tosses about opinions like burning coals, like sharp spears; he flings opinions from here and there like so many hailstones; and as he talks he grows bigger, and his eyes grow larger and the evil in his eyes magnifies. His words are ever more scalding and pointed, and he hems in Reb Zeynvele as with a fence of flaming thorns. Reb Zeynvele feels increasingly fenced in without a chance of escape; he can't catch his breath; and his sons and sons-in-law are equally helpless. No one comes to his assistance. The fence gets tighter and closes in, and Reb Zeynvele begins to feel a hopelessness, a pain in his chest, and his breathing becomes labored. He gets up and goes out the door to catch his breath and to calm himself, for he feels that he is right, that the hunchback is only some kind of trickster, that the hailstones of his arguments can be made to melt and then nothing will be left of them but water. All that is needed is presence of mind.

As we said above, it was a winter night, and as Reb Zeynvele stepped outdoors, the marketplace was covered with freshly fallen sparkling snow, and the heavens above sparkled with an infinite number of stars. Reb Zeynvele breathed deeply, the tightness in his chest loosened, and his brain cleared. Suddenly he looked closely at the fence of thorns with which the hunchback had surrounded him and noticed that it was broken in spots and that here and there it did not hold together. And again he sensed, almost physically, how at these breaks there stood an authority here, a commentator there, signaling to him in a friendly way, calling to him: Zeynvele, the fence about you is a fraud, an illusion! Come, and we will lead you through it; the way out is offering itself to you, the way out of constriction.

Reb Zeynvele smiles at the thought of the way out and becomes aware that everywhere there is spaciousness, a wide-open world. He remembers what this authority said, and what another had done to anticipate doubts; and then he recalls a specific statement in Rashi, and many others. He derives great satisfaction from all this. Once again he retraces his steps through the Talmud and the commentaries—everywhere he finds a free and open world. Now he is going to show up his guest. Everything is clear as the day, shining as the stars in heaven. Meanwhile he is unaware that even as his mind wanders amid universes of learning, his feet lead him through the snow across the marketplace and beyond; that he has long since left the marketplace and is already out of the town. There is not a sign of a house about him, and he tramps in the open, unfenced, and unbounded fields where the clarity and spaciousness matches that in his mind.

All at once he stopped in alarm.

Suddenly, a heavy cloud covered the sky and hid the sparkling stars. A shadow spread over the snow. He felt lost in the snowy fields and his mind, too, lost its way in the questions he was contemplating.

In the distance, Reb Zeynvele noticed some thin smoke curling upward. It must indicate some human habitation. Chilled, weary, and despondent he walked in the direction of the smoke and came to a poor, bedraggled inn. He went in and beheld a smoke-filled room, and he stopped at the door. Nobody noticed him. At the table an old peasant woman drowsed over drink and some refreshments. Through the broken window blew a damp, cold wind. To one side was an oven in which dry chunks of wood crackled as they burned. Tired and frozen as he was, he wanted to go up to the oven to warm himself, but noticed that all the places near it were taken by tipsy peasants holding tin cups of liquor in one hand and herring or pickles in the other. The peasants drank and their faces were flushed with pleasure and good will. Now and then they bent toward each other and kissed and wept out of love for one another, and then they drank again and shared the refreshments.

And Reb Zeynvele, the man who excelled the rabbi in learning, who could sing better than the cantor, who could read the Torah better than the Litvak teacher, who had a skillful wife and fine children, the nicest *sukkah* in town and the handsomest ethrog; the same Reb Zeynvele who was the best counselor, the most honest arbitrator, and who gave the most generous donations to charity, even he lost control of himself, and standing there in the midst of the inn in his overcoat that hung on him as if made of tin whenever the wind stole under it and froze the sweat on his body—at that moment, deep in his heart, Reb Zeynvele envied the peasants who sat by the warm oven drinking liquor, wiping it down with herring and pickles, and talking obscenities.

And there began for him a new series of incarnations.

Translated by Shlomo Katz

The Hermit and the Bear

Once there was a man who could not abide evil. So he turned the little shop he kept over to his wife, shut himself up in a room in his house, and immersed himself in Torah and prayer—studying the revealed scripture and the kabbalah as well.

But even at home, in his very own household, he saw evil. Finally, thinking the matter over, he decided to become a hermit, left his home, and went to study in a corner of the synagogue.

He sits in the synagogue, but the world's evil follows him there. Sometimes a night watchman comes in to warm himself at the stove, or a wanderer comes in to sleep, or a sleepless man blunders into the synagogue—and they sit around the stove talking—but whatever they talk about, the end is always evil upon evil.

Again, the hermit ponders the matter and leaves town to go out into the world to look for a city without evil. And he doesn't find one. It's the same world wherever he goes.

So he gives up on civilization and travels from forest to forest, over hills and valleys until, far from all human habitation, he comes to a stream. What the river is called he does not know, but on its bank there stand the ruins of an ancient palace.

Well, he settles there and busies himself with the kabbalah. But there's no way to escape from evil. The river sometimes runs wild, overturning boats, tearing up hunks of meadow and even newly sown fields. As for what goes on among the fish—a constant warfare.

So the hermit has no peace and cannot sleep. As for running away—there's no place left to run.

He lies there and thinks and thinks, trying to fathom where the source of so much evil might be; and so comes to the conclusion that evil happens because the soul of the world is asleep.

That's not such a wild thought as it seems. For instance, consider the small world of man. So long as a man's soul is awake, he does what is fitting, according to plan and according to reason. All his limbs obey his soul. But when a man is asleep, then the soul—the master of the body—dozes off; and the body starts thrashing about, without order, without purpose. Every limb goes off on its own: one hand here, the other there; the head for itself, the body for itself—all without reason.

One can get badly hurt that way!

And evil is reasonless. The world thrashes, convulsed without order; and the soul of the world is asleep. Every separate bit of the world looks out for itself, not for the welfare of all.

Do you understand? Right or wrong, this is what the hermit thought.

So he concludes that there is only one thing to do: to wake the soul of the world. Once it is awake, then order will reign. The conflicts, the convulsions, the thrashing about of the world's limbs will stop.

But how does one wake the soul of the world? For *that* there are ideas in the holy books. There are certain things to say and to do. It takes some fervent meditation. One has to dedicate oneself to the task wholeheartedly and with devotion. If not, the words fly off into thin air—into nothing.

Clearly, something must be created that has wings and a soul; something that knows where to fly and what to ask for when it gets there. Of course, during the day, it's not possible to create it. No sooner do you get deeply involved in thought, than a crow caws, a bird sings, or one hears a distant peasant cursing the hard soil for dulling his plow.

The right time is at night, especially at midnight.

So that's what the hermit does—night after night until he senses that he's getting somewhere.

But the angry river-spirit becomes aware of what he's doing and says: "No peace for him!" No sooner is the hermit engrossed in his meditation, than the river-spirit flings himself about, making the river seethe and roar and heave its waves against the banks until the hermit's deep thoughts are as topsy-turvy as the boatman overturned down river in the commotion.

The hermit, then, who is not eager to go looking for another ruin beside some other river (Who knows how long that would take or whether he'd find what he's looking for?); the hermit, then, sees that he must move the river, river-spirit and all, because, after all, evil is still multiplying and destroying the world.

Well—moving the river is a small matter for the hermit. He has a holy spell for that. All it takes is some additional fasting, some deep meditation, and the river moves.

Which puts the river-spirit into a fiery rage; but too bad for him. The holy spell has been spoken. And yet, the spirit wants revenge; so he agitates the river even more and makes the waves grow huge. Then, snatching a swollen wave, he flings it toward the bank, toward the ruins.

And the wave turns into a bear. A hairy black bear with bloodshot eyes that runs around the ruins, roaring and snarling, interfering with the hermit's meditations once again.

What's to be done? He's not going to kill the bear. That would be evil. Because, in truth, how is the bear guilty of anything? It lives; let it live!

Well, it occurs to the hermit to quiet the bear. To make something decent of him, so that, bear though he is, he will understand what it's all about.

The hermit decides to elevate the bear. He will change him and enlighten his soul.

So, one morning early, the hermit climbs to the top of his ruin and stands there looking down at the bear. No sooner does the bear see him than he falls into a dreadful rage. Digging the ground with his forepaws, he roars and growls and leaps about, his mouth foaming, glaring with bloodshot eyes at the hermit; and the hermit, his eyes filled with lovingkindness, looks down at the bear. And there's a war between the two sets of eyes—the hermit's brimming with love and pity, the bear's filled with hatred and rage. But the hermit's eyes are the stronger. Slowly, slowly, they begin to conquer those of the bear.

The conflict between the two pairs of eyes, between the two hearts and the two souls, lasts a long time until, when the sun is in the east, the struggle is over; and when it is high in the heavens, the bear lies humbly before the ruin like a submissive dog; and when the sun sets, the bear rises quietly and sends the hermit a tenderly pleading look and approaches the gate of the ruins where it knocks quietly, whining like a dog to be let in.

The hermit has won. The hairy beast has given up, and his whining means to say: "Let me come to you. Let me serve you

like a dog. I'll lie at your feet; I'll lick your hands, and look
faithfully into your eyes, and anticipate your every desire; and
when you are deep in meditation, I'll be nice and quiet beside
you—I won't even catch flies."

The hermit opens the gate. The bear approaches him and lies
down quietly at his feet. And his eyes say: "You are my God. My
hopes are in you. I believe in you. Your thoughts are holy. With
your meditations you will rebuild the world." And the hermit
lovingly caresses the bear, the bear he has himself created, the
bear that believes in him.

And he begins to muse, desiring to be immersed in his
thoughts once more, to meditate on what is needful to wake the
soul of the world.

But there is nothing left for him to think. He himself no longer
possesses his former soul, because in the same measure that the
bear has ascended to him, he has descended to the bear.

He senses a weariness in all his limbs; his eyelids grow heavy.
Falteringly, he goes to his bed, and the bear follows him and lies
down beside him.

There is no end to evil. The bear has become partly human,
and the human, partly a bear. And a saint who lies down with a
bear cannot wake the soul of the world.

Translated by Leonard Wolf

If Not Higher

Early every Friday morning, at the time of the Penitential Prayers, the rabbi of Nemirov would vanish.

He was nowhere to be seen—neither in the synagogue nor in the two Houses of Study nor at a *minyan*. And he was certainly not at home. His door stood open; whoever wished could go in and out; no one would steal from the rabbi. But not a living creature was within.

Where could the rabbi be? Where should he be? In heaven, no doubt. A rabbi has plenty of business to take care of just before the Days of Awe. Jews, God bless them, need livelihood, peace, health, and good matches. They want to be pious and good, but our sins are so great, and Satan of the thousand eyes watches the whole earth from one end to the other. What he sees he reports; he denounces, informs. Who can help us if not the rabbi!

That's what the people thought.

But once a Litvak came, and he laughed. You know the Litvaks. They think little of the Holy Books but stuff themselves with Talmud and law. So this Litvak points to a passage in the Gemara—it sticks in your eyes—where it is written that even Moses our Teacher did not ascend to heaven during his lifetime but remained suspended two and a half feet below. Go argue with a Litvak!

So where can the rabbi be?

"That's not my business," said the Litvak, shrugging. Yet all the while—what a Litvak can do!—he is scheming to find out.

That same night, right after the evening prayers, the Litvak steals into the rabbi's room, slides under the rabbi's bed, and waits. He'll watch all night and discover where the rabbi vanishes and what he does during the Penitential Prayers.

Someone else might have got drowsy and fallen asleep, but a Litvak is never at a loss; he recites a whole tractate of the Talmud by heart.

At dawn he hears the call to prayers.

The rabbi has already been awake for a long time. The Litvak has heard him groaning for a whole hour.

Whoever has heard the rabbi of Nemirov groan knows how much sorrow for all Israel, how much suffering, lies in each groan. A man's heart might break, hearing it. But a Litvak is made of iron; he listens and remains where he is. The rabbi—long life to him!—lies on the bed, and the Litvak under the bed.

Then the Litvak hears the beds in the house begin to creak; he hears people jumping out of their beds, mumbling a few Jewish words, pouring water on their fingernails, banging doors. Everyone has left. It is again quiet and dark; a bit of light from the moon shines through the shutters.

(Afterward the Litvak admitted that when he found himself alone with the rabbi a great fear took hold of him. Goose pimples spread across his skin, and the roots of his earlocks pricked him like needles. A trifle: to be alone with the rabbi at the time of the Penitential Prayers! But a Litvak is stubborn. So he quivered like a fish in water and remained where he was.)

Finally the rabbi—long life to him!—arises. First he does what befits a Jew. Then he goes to the clothes closet and takes out a bundle of peasant clothes: linen trousers, high boots, a coat, a big felt hat, and a long wide leather belt studded with brass nails. The rabbi gets dressed. From his coat pocket dangles the end of a heavy peasant rope.

The rabbi goes out, and the Litvak follows him.

On the way the rabbi stops in the kitchen, bends down, takes an ax from under the bed, puts it in his belt, and leaves the house. The Litvak trembles but continues to follow.

The hushed dread of the Days of Awe hangs over the dark streets. Every once in a while a cry rises from some *minyan* reciting the Penitential Prayers, or from a sickbed. The rabbi hugs the sides of the streets, keeping to the shade of the houses. He glides from house to house, and the Litvak after him. The Litvak hears the sound of his heartbeats mingling with the sound of the rabbi's heavy steps. But he keeps on going and follows the rabbi to the outskirts of the town.

A small wood stands behind the town.

The rabbi—long life to him!—enters the wood. He takes thirty or forty steps and stops by a small tree. The Litvak, overcome with amazement, watches the rabbi take the ax out of his belt and strike the tree. He hears the tree creak and fall. The rabbi chops the tree into logs and the logs into sticks. Then he makes a bundle of the wood and ties it with the rope in his pocket. He puts the bundle of wood on his back, shoves the ax back into his belt, and returns to the town.

He stops at a back street beside a small broken-down shack and knocks at the window.

"Who is there?" asks a frightened voice. The Litvak recognizes it as the voice of a sick Jewish woman.

"I," answers the rabbi in the accent of a peasant.

"Who is I?"

Again the rabbi answers in Russian. "Vassil."

"Who is Vassil, and what do you want?"

"I have wood to sell, very cheap." And, not waiting for the woman's reply, he goes into the house.

The Litvak steals in after him. In the gray light of early morning he sees a poor room with broken, miserable furnishings. A sick woman, wrapped in rags, lies on the bed. She complains bitterly, "Buy? How can I buy? Where will a poor widow get money?"

"I'll lend it to you," answers the supposed Vassil. "It's only six cents."

"And how will I ever pay you back?" asks the poor woman, groaning.

"Foolish one," says the rabbi reproachfully. "See, you are a poor sick Jew, and I am ready to trust you with a little wood. I am sure you'll pay. While you, you have such a great and mighty God and you don't trust him for six cents."

"And who will kindle the fire?" asks the widow. "Have I the strength to get up? My son is at work."

"I'll kindle the fire," answers the rabbi.

As the rabbi put the wood into the oven he recited, in a groan, the first portion of the Penitential Prayers.

As he kindled the fire and the wood burned brightly, he recited, a bit more joyously, the second portion of the Penitential Prayers. When the fire was set he recited the third portion, and then he shut the stove.

The Litvak who saw all this became a disciple of the rabbi.

And ever after, when another disciple tells how the rabbi of Nemirov ascends to heaven at the time of the Penitential Prayers, the Litvak does not laugh. He only adds quietly, "If not higher."

Translated by Marie Syrkin

Three Gifts

At the Scales of Heaven

Ages ago a Jew died somewhere.

Well, a Jew died—one can't live forever. So they gave him his due . . . they brought him to the cemetery.

After the burial, the son said Kaddish—the soul flies up to judgment, to heaven's tribunal.

When it arrives, it finds hanging there in front of the court-room the scales on which good and bad deeds are weighed. The dead man's advocate, his former good angel, appears and, hold-ing a spotless bag white as snow, takes his stand to the right of the scales. The dead man's accuser, his former bad angel, appears and, holding a soiled bag, takes his stand to the left of the scales.

In the spotless white bag are good deeds; in the filthy black bag misdeeds. From the snow-white bag the advocate empties good deeds onto the right-hand scale—deeds that smell like perfumes and gleam like the stars in the sky. From the filthy bag the accuser empties misdeeds onto the left-hand scale—deeds black as coal, with exactly the reek of tar and pitch.

The poor soul stands there, looks, and gapes—it had never imagined that there was such a difference between "good" and "bad." Quite often, down there, it had failed to recognize them, mistaking one for the other.

The scales lift slowly, up and down, first one, then the other. The arrow quivers, leftward by a hair, rightward by a hair.

Only by a hair . . . and no sudden shifting! He had been a simple man, neither especially malicious nor especially saintlike; thus—tiny good deeds, tiny misdeeds, scraps, motes of dust, at times barely visible to the naked eye.

Yet, when the arrow moves rightward by a hair, there rings through the halls of heaven a sound of joy, of satisfaction; when, alas, it moves leftward, a sigh tears loose and rises to the Judg-ment Seat.

And the angels empty their bags slowly, solemnly. Speck by speck, particle by particle, the way simple folk auction prayers, penny by penny.

But even a well runs dry; at last the bags are empty.

"Is that it?" asks the court *shammes*, also an angel among angels.

Both good and evil spirits turn their bags upside down: there's no more! The *shammes* comes forward to see where the arrow has stopped: to the right or to the left. He looks and looks, and sees something that has never happened since heaven and earth were created.

"What's taking so long?" asks the chief judge.

The *shammes* stammers, "Even! The arrow stands at dead center! The bad deeds weigh the same as the good."

"Exactly the same?" Again a question from the judgment table.

The *shammes* takes another look and answers, "To a hair!"

The tribunal deliberates, and hands down its verdict: "Since the bad deeds do not outweigh the good, the soul does not belong in hell. On the other hand, the good deeds do not outweigh the bad, therefore one cannot open the gates of paradise.

"Let it wander aimlessly. Let it fly around in mid-air, between heaven and earth, till God reminds Himself of it and takes pity, and beckons it unto Him in His mercy."

And the *shammes* takes the soul and leads it out.

The soul, alas, moans and groans at its fate.

"Why are you crying?" asks the *shammes*. "You won't have the pleasure and joy of heaven, but neither will you have the anguish and grief of hell. Fair and square!"

But the soul refuses to be comforted. "Better the greatest anguish," it says, "than *nothing*! *Nothing* is horrible!"

The *shammes* of heaven's tribunal takes pity, and offers a way out. "Fly down, little soul," he says, "and hover close to the world of the living.

"Don't look up into the heavens," he says. "What would you see on the other side? Only the stars, bright but cold creatures; they know nothing of mercy; they won't care about you; they won't remind God of you. . . .

"Only the saints of paradise can care about a poor, outcast soul. And they—listen carefully—they love gifts . . . beautiful gifts. That," he adds bitterly, "is the way saints are nowadays!

"So fly, little soul," he continues, "hover close to the world of the living and see how life is, see what's happening. And if you see something unusually beautiful and good, seize it and fly up with it; it will be a gift for the saints in paradise. And with the gift in your hand, knock and announce yourself in my name to the sentinel angel. Say I told you to!

"And when you've brought three gifts, rest assured—the gates of paradise will open to you, the gifts will do their work. At God's seat it is not the well-born who are loved, but those who've come up the hard way. . . ."

And with these words he pushes the soul gently out of heaven.

The First Gift

So the poor soul flies about, hovering close to the world of the living, and seeks gifts for the saints in paradise. It flies everywhere, over villages and cities, ignoring not the smallest settlement—amid blazing rays in the most intense heat; during the rainy season—amid drops and needle showers; at summer's end—amid silver cobwebs that hang in the air; in winter—amid the snowflakes that fall from on high. It looks and looks and looks its eyes out.

Wherever it sees a Jew, it quickly flies down and looks him in the eyes: Is he on his way to the synagogue to cleanse his soul?

Wherever a light glimmers at night through a crack in a shutter, the soul is there: Are God's fragrant flowers—those unadvertised good deeds—growing in the silent house?

Alas! most of the time it jumps back from eyes and windows, aghast and shuddering.

And as the seasons and years pass, the soul almost sinks into despair. Cities have turned into cemeteries, cemeteries are ploughed into fields; woods have been hacked away, stones at the water's edge turned into sand, rivers changed their beds, thousands of stars fallen, millions of souls risen—and His Beloved Name has not reminded Himself of the wandering one, and it has found nothing unusually good and beautiful.

The soul thinks: The world is so poor, the people so mediocre and gray-souled, and their deeds are so petty. What can possibly be unusual in such lives? I am doomed to eternal wandering and exile!

But as it thinks these thoughts, a red flame bursts forth before its eyes—in the middle of the dark, heavy night, a red flame. It looks around. The flame bursts from a high window.

Thieves have attacked a rich man, thieves with masks on their faces. One holds a burning torch and lights the room; another puts a flashing knife to the rich man's breast and keeps saying: "Move, Jew, and you're finished! The point of the knife goes through your back!" The others ransack chests and drawers.

But the Jew stands at knife-point and looks on calmly; not one hair of the brows over his clear eyes, not one hair of the white beard that reaches to his loins, can be seen to stir. No concern of his. The Lord giveth, the Lord taketh away, he thinks; blessed be the name of the Lord! "One isn't born with wealth, one doesn't take it to the grave," his pale lips whisper.

And he looks on quite undisturbed, as they open the last drawer of the last chest and drag out bags of gold and silver, bags of jewels, and all sorts of precious ware. He is silent. Maybe he is renouncing them all!

Suddenly, when the thieves come upon the last hiding place and draw forth a little bag, the last and best hidden, he forgets himself, he is all atremble, his eyes flame, he stretches forth his right hand, preparing to scream: "Don't touch that!"

But in place of a scream a red jet of smoking blood spurts out—the knife has done its job. It is the blood of his heart and it spurts onto the bag. He falls and the robbers swiftly tear open the bag—the best, the most precious of his treasures will be here!

But they've made a bitter mistake; they've spilled blood for nothing—no silver, no gold, no jewelry is in the bag; nothing worth a high price in this world! There is only a bit of earth, earth from the Holy Land intended for his grave, and it was this the rich man tried to rescue from the hands and eyes of strangers and spattered with his blood.

The soul seizes a blood-soaked speck of earth from the Holy Land and appears at the little window of heaven.

Its first gift is accepted.

The Second Gift

"Remember," the angel calls, locking the window of heaven behind it, "two more gifts!"

"With God's help!" the soul hopes, and flies merrily down.

But in time its happiness ceases. Again years and years go by, and the soul sees nothing unusually beautiful. Gloomy thoughts again attack it: like a living well-spring, the world has broken loose from God's will, and runs and keeps running through the ages. And the longer it runs, the more earth and dust it incorporates; the muddier, filthier it becomes; one finds fewer gifts worthy of heaven. The people grow pettier, their good deeds drabber, their sins dirtier, their actions invisible to the naked eye!

If God, the soul continues, were suddenly to command that the good deeds and sins of the whole world be put on the scales, the arrow would also scarcely budge, just barely quiver.

The world too can go neither down nor up, it too is a wanderer between the radiant heaven and the dark abyss . . . and its advocate and accuser would battle over it forever, as light and darkness, warm and cold, life and death forever battle here.

The world rocks back and forth, and it can't—can't go up, can't go down; and because of this there will forever be weddings and divorces, births and funerals, days of celebration and of mourning, and love and hate . . . forever, forever.

Suddenly, a clamor of trumpets and bugles. The soul looks down: a German city (naturally, a medieval one); all sorts of gabled roofs surround the square, and the square swarms with people decked in many colors; faces crowd the windows; people are on the roofs; some sit astride the beams that jut out of the walls under the roofs; the balconies burst with onlookers.

In front of the courthouse stands a table, covered by a green cloth with golden fringes and tassels. At the table sit the gentlemen of the court in velvet robes with golden clasps, and sable caps with white feathers fastened by brilliant studs. At the head of the table the president sits. A ravenous eagle flutters over his head.

A Jewish girl, bound hand and foot, stands to one side. Nearby ten underlings restrain a wild horse. The president rises and reads the verdict from a parchment. And he turns his face to the marketplace: "This Jewess here, this daughter of the Jews, has committed a grievous sin, a grievous sin which even God, for all His mercy, could not forgive. She stole out of the ghetto during our recent holy day, and walked through our clean streets. And with her shameless eyes she defiled our sacred procession, our sacred images that we carried through the streets with hymns of praise and kettledrums. With her accursed ears she drank the chanting of our white-clad, innocent children and the beating of the sacred drums. And who knows whether the

Devil, the foul fiend, taking the shape of this Jewish daughter, got up close and defiled one of our holy things?

"What did he want, the Devil, inside this beautiful shape? For I can't deny it—she *is* beautiful, beautiful as only a devil can make her. Look at the eyes flashing proudly from under their modestly downcast silken lashes! Look at the alabaster face that has grown paler, but not less fair, through long imprisonment! Look at her fingers, her long, slender fingers; the sun glows through them!

"This is what he wanted, the Devil, to tear a soul away from the ecstasy of the procession. And his scheme worked. 'What a beauty!' cried one of the knights, a member of a most distinguished family. And this was too much. The guards noticed her and seized her. He didn't even resist, the Devil—and why? Because at that moment they were cleansed of all sin; he had no power over them.

"And this is our judgment against the Devil in the shape of the Jewish girl: Let her be tied by the hair, by the long, devilish braids, to the tail of this wild horse. Let it run and drag her like a carcass through the streets which her feet have trodden in defiance of our sacred decree. Let her blood splatter and wash clean the stones which she has defiled with her feet!"

A shriek of joy explodes from every mouth, and when the uproar subsides the doomed girl is asked whether she has a final wish.

"Yes," she answers calmly, "I would like a few pins."

"She's crazed with fear!" the gentlemen of the court believe.

"No!" she answers quietly and coldly. "This is my final wish and request."

Her request is granted.

"And now," the president commands, "tie her up!"

Guards approach and with trembling hands they bind the long black braids of the rabbi's daughter to the tail of the wild horse, which by now can scarcely be restrained.

"Make room!" the president commands the multitude in the square. A tumult. People move aside and press against the walls of the houses; and all raise their hands, some with whips, some with pikes, some with knotted handkerchiefs; and all are eager to goad the wild horse; everyone holds his breath; all faces are aflame; all eyes flash. In the uproar no one notices that the doomed one is stooping quietly, pinning the hem of her dress to her feet and sticking the pins deep, deep into her flesh so that her body will not be exposed when the horse drags her through the streets.

It is noticed only by the wandering one—the soul.

"Let go of the horse!" the president commands, and his underlings leap aside, and it suddenly tears loose. From every mouth there also tears loose a cry. All the whips, pikes, and handkerchiefs whistle in the air. And in wild terror the horse plunges across the marketplace, through streets and back streets, out, out of town.

But the soul, the wandering one, has already drawn a blood-stained pin from the doomed girl's foot and hurries up to heaven with it.

"Only one more gift!" the angel at the little window comforts the wanderer.

The Third Gift

The soul flies down again; it needs only one more gift.

And once again seasons and years go by, and once again it is stricken by despair. The world seems to have grown even pettier, the people pettier, their deeds pettier—the good as well as the bad.

One day a thought comes to the soul: If God, praised be His Name, would decide to stop the world suddenly, once and for all, and judge it, just as it is; and if an advocate would take his stand on one side and shake specks and particles out of a white bag, and on the opposite side the Accuser would shake out his bits and pieces, a long, long time would pass before the bags would be emptied . . . so many petty things, so many!

But once the bags were empty, what would happen? The arrow would surely stop at dead center! With such petty things, so many petty things, nothing can tip the scales. And why? One more little feather, one more little straw, one more bit of chaff, one more speck of dust!

And what would God do? How would He sentence the world? Back to chaos? No. The bad deeds don't outweigh the good. Redemption? Not that either. The good deeds don't outweigh the bad. What then?

"Go on!" He would say. "Fly on between hell and heaven, love and hate, compassionate tears and streaming blood, between cradles and graves. Keep going, keep going!"

The soul, however, was destined to be redeemed. From these melancholy thoughts a sound of drums awakes it.

What place is this? What century?

The soul recognizes neither the place nor the time, but it sees a prison yard. The sunbeams move playfully along the iron grates in the little windows. They also slip in among the weapons stacked along the wall. The soldiers have just been handed switches. They've been placed in two long rows, with a narrow passage between.

Some little Jew with a torn shirt on his emaciated body, a *yarmulke* on his half-shaven head, is brought forward.

What is he being punished for? Who knows; it happened in bygone times! Maybe a theft, maybe a robbery or a murder, and maybe a frameup. After all, in bygone times.

The soldiers smile and wonder: Why have they taken so many of us and lined us up? He won't last halfway! But now they thrust him in, between the rows; now he's on his way, and he walks steadily and does not stumble and does not fall. He takes the blows and endures them.

Frenzy seizes the soldiers. He's still on his feet, still walking. The whips whistle in the air like devils and coil around his body like snakes. The blood spurts and spurts from his emaciated form, and doesn't stop spurting!

In the midst of this a soldier swings too high and knocks the *yarmulke* off the condemned man's head. A few steps and the prisoner notices it. He stops short, as if a thought has struck him. He mulls it over and turns around. He will not go bareheaded! He returns to the spot where the *yarmulke* lies, he bends down and picks it up, and turns around again and goes on, calmly —bloodied red, but with the *yarmulke* on his head. He goes until he falls.

And when he fell, the soul flew close and caught up the *yarmulke* that had cost so many useless blows, and took it up to the little window of heaven.

And the third gift was also accepted!

And the saints interceded for the soul. In consideration of its three gifts the gates of paradise opened to it.

And the Eternal Voice declared: "Truly beautiful gifts, unusually beautiful. . . . They have no practical value, no use at all, but as far as beauty is concerned—unusual."

Translated by Aaron Kramer

The Shabbes-Goy *

1.
Pleasures of the snuffbox.
All sorts of teeth.
A mouthwash.

The Chelmer rabbi, in ragged fur cap and tattered satin robe, a tiny Jew with a prominent Adam's apple and laughing gray eyes in a shrivelled face. . . . Between one talmudic problem and the next, the cheerful, gray-headed rabbi gets up, surveys with confidence the open Gemara through glasses on the tip of his nose, his shawl popping out of his chest, and as his rightful share of worldly pleasures, takes up the wooden snuffbox.

A soft-hearted person, a being contented with his lot, he smiles at the snuffbox and taps on the cover, drumming lightly with his small fingers as though asking: Is there a little something there?

And when the snuffbox replies softly, "There is a bit left, there is!" he opens it leisurely, takes a crumb of a morsel between his fingertips and brings it to his nostrils, presses gently to the right, gently to the left—and then again. His eyes brighten, his heart gladdens, he strolls about the House of Judgment almost dancing, and gives praise to the world's Creator in singsong: "*Ai, ai, Gottenyu*, dear God, what a sweet world you have created!"

"What splendid creatures walk about in your dear world! Jews, and—to be exact—others. *Ai*, people made of gold, of velvet, of satin . . ."

Suddenly someone drops in: "Rebbe, help!"

He is alarmed.

"What happened to you, Yankele? *Yankele!*"

*A *Shabbes-goy* is a non-Jew hired to do small chores forbidden to Jews on the Sabbath, such as lighting candles.

Chelm is the name of an ancient Jewish town in Poland, one of those destroyed by the Holocaust; in the folklore of the East European Jews it also became known as a "town of fools," and there is a rich body of humorous stories about the Jews of Chelm.

He recognizes him. The rabbi knows everyone in Chelm, for he has been godfather to almost all. And when he sees Yankele's bloodied mouth: "*Oi*, Yankele, who wronged you so, Yankele?"

Yankele is already seated on the bench in front of the table of justice holding on to his cheeks with blood-stained hands and rocking away without stopping, from left to right, this way and that.

"*Oi*, Yankele, who wronged you so, Yankele?"

"*Oi, oi,* the *Shabbes-goy*, Rebbe."

The Chelmer rabbi stares in amazement. "In the middle of the week, how do you come to the *Shabbes-goy*, Yankele?"

"A destined thing, Rebbe Leyb. I'm walking as usual in the marketplace. Just walking. And do you think, Rebbe Leyb, that I have the *Shabbes-goy* in mind? I have nothing else to think about but the *Shabbes-goy*? A Jew thinks about making a living, that's what he thinks about. Soon I'll be going home with empty hands—and I don't stop worrying. What will my wife have to say? That shrew of mine . . . but you know her well, Rebbe Leyb! So he comes toward me, the *Shabbes-goy*, and I look and see he's eating pumpkin seeds . . . and with such skill! He throws a handful right into his mouth—a single crack and already he's spitting out the shells, to the right and to the left. So I stop and observe this great dexterity.

"He becomes friendly, like an equal, and says, 'Yankele, come on, open your mouth, Yankele!'

"Well, seeing that a *goy* pleads, I open my mouth supposing, *Rebbenyu*, dear Rebbe, that he wants to throw some nuts into it. I open wide . . . so he takes his fist, and—bang! Right into my mouth!"

"At this, Yankele starts crying afresh: "*Oi*, the murderer, the murderer . . ."

But this does not please the Chelmer rabbi at all. He draws nearer and reproaches him: "That I don't like, Yankele. How can you say such a thing, just so, about one of God's creatures—*murderer*?"

"But take a look, he knocked out three of my teeth," sobs Yankele, and shows him the teeth.

The rabbi looks closely, shakes his head and says incredulously, "Tell me the truth, Yankele, are these *your* teeth?"

"Whose then, Rebbe? Here, Rebbe, look!"

The rabbi looks and marvels.

And Yankele opens his mouth wide to show him the holes.

"Wonder of wonders," says the rabbi after a pause, "that a Jew should have such teeth. . . ."

"What kind of teeth, then, should a Jew have," asks Yankele, by this time alarmed.

"Here, look!" answers the rabbi and shows him the old "furniture" in his aged mouth. "Some have no teeth at all—in any case, not *such* teeth! After all, I wasn't born yesterday. Never have I seen such teeth in a Jew's mouth!"

And the rabbi proceeds to ponder two questions at once: How does a Jew come to have such large, strong teeth? As to the *Shabbes-goy*, what impels him to knock out strange teeth?

He ponders and ponders, and then jumps up. "Aha! That is to say, solved!

"It's all very clear, Yankele! The one depends upon the other. Just like that, you say *murderer*. About one of God's creatures, *murderer*? There's no such thing. If there were murderers in the world, would God permit the world to exist? So what then? But since you are relating an incident that happened, after all, and I believe you, and I see with my own eyes the knocked-out teeth, I must conclude, you understand, thus . . ."

He pauses to catch his breath and expounds: "The guilt, Yankele, in reality belongs to your teeth!"

Yankele leaps up to his full height. "How is it possible, Rebbe—my *teeth*? And the *goy*?"

"Wholly innocent he is not, Yankele, that's not what I'm saying! The basic fault, however, lies in the teeth; that is to say, not *your* teeth. . . ."

"What do you mean?"

"Listen with attention, Yankele! By nature the *goy* is an amiable creature . . . he was eating pumpkin seeds, he saw you, he really wanted to be hospitable and give you some . . . so, 'Open your mouth!' he says . . . and wants to throw nuts into it—after all, they're fond of doing favors and little tricks . But when you, Yankele, obeyed and he saw such fine teeth, that is to say, *his teeth in your mouth* . . . you understand, a *goy*, and his teeth in your mouth, so naturally he becomes excited. And since he's a *goy*, what else can he do when he gets excited? So he hits out with his fist.

"Do as I tell you, Yankele," the rabbi concludes, "don't make a fuss about it. . . . Go home to your wife and tell her I told you, that I explicitly told you, she should make you a mouthwash out of figs. . . ."

As Yankele submissively departs the rabbi calls after him: "And the next time a *goy* tells you to open your mouth, open just a little bit, not more than a bit—a crack! He doesn't have to see anything, that a Jew has teeth. . . ."

2.
*More blows. The rabbi
offers to pray for a
half-loaf of bread.
Good advice.*

The Chelmer rabbi returns to his books, studies with gusto, and derives much joy from the holy Torah—and from time to time helps himself to a pinch of worldly paradise from the wooden snuffbox. His heart expands with joy!

"*Oi*, a dear world, a sweet world. . . ." And he glances again through the ancient, moldy pane of the House of Judgment's narrow window into the marketplace.

"Such precious people, *Gottenyu*, silky, satiny. . . ." But he does not finish his praises, for here comes Yankele again. A full month has not yet elapsed.

The rabbi stares in wonder. "What I dreamed last night, just the other night. . . . What happened this time, Yankele?"

"The *Shabbes-goy*, Rebbe! The *Shabbes-goy* again!" yells Yankele, and collapses on the bench.

Benignly the rabbi scolds him, "What a pest you are, Yankele! Still bothering with the *Shabbes-goy*? A murderer, God forbid, he's not, but what do you need him for?"

"He stole up on me from behind," explains Yankele, "*from behind*, Rebbe Leyb! I'm walking through the alley, I'm on my way home . . . I'm carrying a loaf of bread for my family, I bought a loaf of bread for my wife and little ones, his Dear Name destined a loaf for me! Under my arm I'm carrying it when suddenly, from behind, a blow on my head. I fall down, I faint, I've scarcely come to . . . and I see the *Shabbes-goy* walking away with a full mouth, chewing—and the loaf of bread lies at my feet, bitten off. Here, look, *Rebbenyu*. *Oi*, my head, my head!"

He shows the rabbi the loaf and grabs his head.

The rabbi examines the bread and says, "The head is a triviality; from a blow, God forbid, one doesn't perish! But consider, Yankele, who was in the right? Here, take a look—*teeth!* A *goy*, as you see, has teeth! Do you see? One bite, and half a loaf gone at once! *I* couldn't do it!"

"Yes, Rebbe," admits Yankele, "but what's to be done with the murderer? All Chelm is in danger!"

"And don't think, Yankele," the rabbi turns to him, "that I'm not suffering on account of this. I know what half a loaf of bread means to a person like you, with so many mouths in your house to feed, I know what it means. Alas, there won't be enough to go round. If it depended on me, and I tell you this in confidence, I would positively request that the community compensate you for half a loaf. Why not? True, the community is poor, but still, a Jew has suffered a loss from *everybody's Shabbes-goy*. And half a loaf is not merely blows . . . the community wouldn't be impoverished . . . but you know yourself, Yankele, that I have no say."

Yankele starts screaming, "So that's how it is? It means only one thing—there is no judge and there is no justice in this world . . . the murderer goes about scot-free!"

"Murderer," replies the rabbi serenely, "is not necessarily the proper word. I explained that to you once before, if it were so; the world would not be permitted to exist. There are no murderers!"

"So what then?"

"The guilt, I tell you, Yankele, lies in the bread. In the holy books it is written: 'A man sins because of bread.' You know the small print yourself. 'A man sins on account of a crumb of bread.' And all the books say that there are times when a Jew transgresses the commandment 'Thou shalt not covet'—sometimes even 'Thou shalt not steal.' A *goy*, to make a distinction, may transgress 'Thou shalt not steal'—sometimes even 'Thou shalt not kill.' But this, too, however, not by nature. It's all the fault of the bread. You have no idea, Yankele, of the evil impulse that lies hidden in bread. Basically—now tell me your opinion frankly, Yankele—why should it exasperate the *Shabbes-goy* when he sees that Yankele walks about on the street, feeds his little ones, and praises God? Hah? But when he sees *bread*, that Yankele is carrying a loaf of bread! Yes, Yankele—I see you comprehend me now. Chew it well!"

And the rabbi goes over to him, puts his arm about Yankele's shoulder, and says with great compassion, "You know what, Yankele? After all, you know that I am a humble person, by nature a humble person, and I don't like to do such things . . . however, I will do it for you, for your sake. I will pray to God especially for half a loaf on your account."

"Thanks, *Rebbenyu!*" Yankele jumps up overjoyed and starts to leave the hut.

But the rabbi detains him. "Listen carefully, Yankele. Don't ever carry bread exposed and uncovered that his Dear Name has destined for you! It is forbidden to tempt the evil impulse. You have a coat—cover it!"

3.
*A spouse with a poker.
Incident in the rear of
the bath.*

A pacified Yankele takes leave of the rabbi and, after a short while, returns for the third time with a cry for help; again the *Shabbes-goy.*

"It is now beyond comprehension," says the rabbi, "that in the course of a single season a Jew should meet with the *Shabbes-goy* three times—and three times get beaten up! It doesn't stand to reason.

"There's something more to this than meets the eye!" he says, wrinkling his forehead, and proceeding to cross-examine. "Did you show him the teeth?"

"God forbid, Rebbe! Since you told me not to!"

Did you keep the bread uncovered?"

"What bread, when bread, Rebbe?"

Ah, if he'd only had bread, he would not have come to this pass. He was on his way home without bread . . . his wife had met him with the poker . . . so he ran away, she ran after him . . . he ran beyond the town to the bathhouse . . . a Jewish wife doesn't run outside the town . . . finally he reaches safety on the slope behind the bath where the *Shabbes-goy* is reclining on the grass. He jumps up and wants to kill Yankele. With his bare fists he'll kill him dead, he says, and punches away. He could barely tear himself away. . . .

"Do you know what, Yankele?" the rabbi says softly after a

contemplative pause, "you will forgive me, but I don't believe you."

Yankele pulls off his coat. "Rebbe, I wish you pieces of gold as big as the blue marks I have. . . ."

And he wants to disrobe completely, but this the rabbi does not permit.

"Little fool, that's not what I mean," says the rabbi. "It's not the least bit necessary to undress. I'm only acting in harmony with my conviction. I can't possibly believe that the *Shabbes-goy*, one of God's creatures after all, should, just like that, without a reason, be a murderer. The concept lacks reality. Tell me, Yankele, does it make sense—a murderer? Could you be a murderer?"

"No!"

"Nor I," says the rabbi.

He falls into a trance, and after a while comes to. "A-ha! That is to say, solved!" and he breaks into a smile. "You know what, Yankele? Listen carefully to what I have to say!"

And he stands up, the better to savor each of his words.

"I tell you, Yankele, in the rear of the bath must be the place where Cain, as it says in the holy Torah, killed his brother Abel. The place itself, more or less, is capable of murder, but particularly is it a dangerous spot for an 'offspring of Noah' who cannot by nature control himself."

Yankele opens mouth and ears. "Ah!"

"What do you say?" smiles the rabbi. "It makes sense? Apparently, that's how it is! And I maintain that the *goy* doesn't even know he is guilty.

"So listen to me, Yankele, and forget about the whole thing! If you wish, call an apothecary; if not, apply cold compresses yourself.

"And on the Sabbath—it's true I don't mix in community matters, but still in times of danger—on the Sabbath, God willing, I will announce in the synagogue and in the House of Study that everyone should avoid going to the rear of the bath.

"And perhaps the council will decide to move the entire bath into town, into the marketplace. Why not? Wouldn't it be better? But that's already outside my sphere. A good day to you, Yankele."

4.
The town meeting. Yankele
must depart. Afterword.

Hardly a month had gone by when Yankele showed up again.

He had no teeth to exhibit, he hadn't been to the rear of the bath, but he did have broken bones. The *Shabbes-goy* had come upon him behind the synagogue.

This time the rabbi had to admit: "What a bandit! Indeed, quite a bandit!" And "A peril for all of Chelm. . . . For me personally, no. I hardly ever step outside the door of my house. . . . Why should I? But, the rest of Chelm!

"Why," he queries, "how are you in greater danger than any other Chelmer? *Your* name is Yankel, another is called Groinem. It has nothing to do with the name. And I don't even know if the *Shabbes-goy* is acquainted with people's names—how that one is called, whose candlesticks he is taking down. . . .

"We must," he sighs, "call a meeting right away, yes. . . . And do you know for what purpose? Can you guess my fear, Yankele?"

"What, Rebbe?"

"On Yom Kippur, when the *goy* comes into the synagogue to light the candles before the final prayer, he can destroy all of Chelm. He can at that moment, God forbid, wipe out the entire community at once!"

And with the Chelmer rabbi it's this way: when he comes to a decision, he acts without delay.

On the Sabbath, in all the houses of prayer, large signs with glaring letters are already hanging: "A MEETING WILL BE HELD! THE WHOLE TOWN IS IN DANGER!"

Danger? The notables gather, the ordinary citizens come running, they sit packed together, cheek by jowl.

"Now tell us everything, what's it about, Rebbe Leyb. . . ."

"Let Yankele say," says he.

So Yankel tells his story. Then the rabbi tells how the supposition was revealed to him . . . but that, nevertheless, Yankele is in the right throughout.

"A murderer," yells Yankele, "a murderer!"

"So what's to be done, *Rebbenyu?*"

The rabbi does not keep them in suspense and speaks as follows. "Were I," he says, "to have a say in the community . . . if I were to be asked in all sincerity, this is what I would say: In the first place, and before anything else—to satisfy the Divine Name—in fact, right away, tomorrow before dawn, Yankele should go away, someplace else . . . because on him the *Shabbes-goy* has a claim already . . . more than a claim—a *fixation*.

"Now, in order to appease his resentment, and with the object of redeeming the entire community from dire peril, let us give the *Shabbes-goy* a raise: a larger portion of the Sabbath loaf and *two* drinks of brandy instead of one. And what else? Perhaps he'll have compassion!"

You're laughing?
Still, there's a little of the Chelmer rabbi in each of us.

Translated by Etta Blum

A Pinch of Snuff

Amiably—moderating his benign smile with a lazy yawn —Satan sat ruffling through the ledger of living souls. Abruptly he stopped. The page of the rabbi of Chelm had fallen open—and it was blank.

Satan's shout raised a swarm of devils: "Find out how much time we have!"

Moments later, they reported back. The life of the rabbi of Chelm hung by a thread.

"Send in my secretary!"

Bald, his eyes red as beets, the secretary romped in. Teetering on thin chicken legs, he winked to his right, smirked to his left, and squatted in the hot pitch bubbling from the floor, folding one spindleshank under the other, Turkish style. Out of one pocket he plucked a fresh crow's feather and a flask of blood drained from an adulterer; out of the other a sheet of skin pared from the back of an atheist. Poised to write, the secretary spit into his hand and bowed toward Satan. "Ready!"

Settling into his armchair, Satan dictated. The secretary clamped his tongue between his teeth, and the crow's quill rasped rapidly across the parchment. The message to the Supreme Authority read: "Since it is written that no man is pure in virtue and free of sin . . . and there lives a rabbi whose days are numbered and whose page of vice remains untouched . . . in order to preserve the integrity of Holy Writ Satan requests jurisdiction over the rabbi of Chelm. . . ."

The answer came back quickly: "Be guided by the first chapter of Job."

Satan understood. In the struggle for the soul of the rabbi, he was not to endanger his life.

But Satan faced obstacles.

The rabbi was a widower, his children married. Ezekiel's decree shielded the children: "The father shall not die for the errors of his sons." Unlike Job, the rabbi maintained neither flocks of sheep nor herds of cattle; he didn't own as much as a milk goat! Only rashes did the rabbi have to spare; the poor man was chafing and scratching himself constantly. How could one afflict the rabbi of Chelm?

"Just a hint of passion," Satan sighed hopefully. He reached for the bell made from the skull of a skeptic, and the devils surged into the room.

"Who will lure the rabbi of Chelm into temptation?"

"I will! I will!"

Each devil knew that a frolic such as this could make his reputation grow like yeast. Volunteering grew so keen that Satan decreed the drawing of lots to avoid mayhem. The two devils who won melted away before they could be wished "good luck."

Jews gravitated to the marketplace because the day was crisp, and because there was nothing else to do. They stood in clusters, appraising the value of the prince's standing timber, and buying and selling skins of rabbits not yet caught and eggs not yet laid. Without warning, the earth shuddered, thunder lashed and rolled—and out of the firebolt a buggy appeared. Wheels clattering, horses slavering, the wagon bowled through the marketplace. The driver—in a fur hat with earflaps, a red sash ringing his hips—leaned back, jerking the reins. The bits dug into the horses' mouths and they reared and whickered in rage. The passenger, a Jew wearing a new caftan, stood up, clutching a bullwhip. He spun out the rawhide, snapping it with a sharp crack over the heads of the span. The team jolted into the traces and lunged across the marketplace, the buggy rattling behind. The Jew in the caftan, still standing, battered the driver's shoulders with his free fist, and let out a piercing whistle whenever the team slowed.

Over the clatter of hooves striking showers of sparks from the ground, the driver bellowed: "Jews! Save me!"

Frightened, a few Jews followed the careening wagon; others turned away to recite the blessing for escaping danger; women ran from shops, terrified.

As the buggy bolted past the slaughterhouse, the butcher's hounds attacked, snapping at fetlocks and muzzles. The horses slowed; a slaughterer snared the bridle and brought the panicked team to a standstill.

A crowd gathered. The well-dressed passenger—straightening his leather money belt—muttered that he had a shepherd for a driver, who would rather graze than press his horses, but the price of diamonds didn't stand still while ponies cropped grass.

Since no one in Chelm had ever seen a diamond, no one disagreed. Surprisingly, the driver nodded in accord. The true problem, he argued, was that the passenger was the driver, and he was the passenger. Last night in the forest the driver had drawn a knife, held it to his throat, changed clothes, and helped himself to horse, buggy, and diamonds. The passenger—or was he the driver?—denied the story of the driver—or was he the passenger?—in its length and in its breadth.

The slaughterer holding the bridle clucked to the horses and, followed by the crowd, led the way to the rabbi.

The rabbi gave each man a private hearing.

The man dressed as a driver sounded like one. Neither the voice nor the vernacular—sturdy as the forest and open as the sky—had ever been heard in a synagogue choir.

Nevertheless, the rabbi questioned him: "How much are the diamonds worth?"

"Rabbi, I'm not very good at figures. Details bore me. But the Lord's been kind, and diamonds I've been able to buy for less and sell for more."

"If I may ask—is the amount of cash in your money belt a detail?"

"No, Rabbi. A blessing, but the Lord frowns on counting——"

Hardly spoken like a plutocrat. The rabbi groaned and sent for the second man.

An intelligent face. The rabbi cited Hillel. The stranger quoted Shammai. Before the rabbi could respond, the stranger untied a bag from his belt and sluiced diamonds and gold coins across the table. "Rabbi, why waste time? Find for me, and I'll forget to count by half when I leave."

The rabbi rose to his feet, shouting, "Thief!"

The crowd rushed in.

No thief. No gold nor diamonds. And outside, no buggy, and no trace of either passenger or driver.

Chelm wondered: Had they been visited by magicians or sorcerers?

The two devils didn't understand why their plan had miscarried.

"Blockheads," Satan explained. "A bribe must remain a secret. Did you expect the rabbi to pay for his Sabbath meal with diamonds? He isn't feeble-minded."

Satan sentenced the two ineffectual devils to be embedded for one year in a block of salt.

When Satan rang the bell made from the skull of a skeptic, the devils clustered around him again—but this time there were no volunteers. Satan waited, then assigned one devil noted for his experience and a second celebrated for his cunning.

After the New Year, before the Day of Atonement, the sky was smudged like smoke and the rain chronic. Sloshing into Chelm along the road running mud, a Jew appeared, a rack of bones, unsteady on his crutches. One foot dragging, he hobbled from house to house and from store to store. At every tenth house he picked up a worn kopeck that slipped through his feeble fingers; at every twentieth he was doled out a crust of bread that he lacked the teeth to eat.

Chelm was not short of beggars. Among its own, Chelm claimed widows and orphans of beadles, rabbis, saints, and water-carriers.

Hour after hour the newcomer trudged through Chelm, numb with cold, the lining of his coat hanging loose, his eyes sinking into their sockets.

Then one day, in the center of the marketplace, he toppled over. He thrashed about in the muck, twitched, and lay still, saliva dribbling from his open mouth.

Jews flocked to the beggar. One sloshed water over his face, another pried open his jaws with a knife so that a third could trickle in raisin wine. A few wailed, "Chelm has become Sodom"—and meanwhile the beggar was expiring.

Someone observed that no Jew should die in the mud. Everyone agreed, but not one offered his home. A few drifted off, and as the crowd began to thin, the rabbi appeared and said, "Take him to me!"

Never had he been obeyed so willingly.

The beggar, still in a coma, was stretched out on the rabbi's bed. The rabbi, seated at his desk reading, glanced up between lines at the sick man. Outside, Jews milled about, waiting for the beggar's end.

At nightfall, as the rabbi prepared for the evening prayer, he heard a moan. Alarmed, he bent over the sick man.

"Rabbi, I'm a sinner. I wish to confess before I die."

The rabbi turned to summon witnesses, but the beggar reached up and clutched his arm.

"God forbid. I'm too ashamed."

Since childhood he'd been a beggar. He'd had few peers—but he'd been dishonest. He'd begged for dowries for daughters he'd never brought to life; for a wife he had yet to meet. He'd solicited money to support students in talmudic academies that didn't exist, and had even sold soil from the Holy Land that he'd dredged up from behind a nearby fence.

Reaching under the rags covering his chest, the beggar drew out a linen pouch and said, "Here it is. Bank notes. Hundreds! For alms . . . for anything. . . ."

The beggar pulled himself closer and wheezed in the rabbi's ear, "Anything, rabbi. Anything. *It's all yours.*"

As if he were fifty years younger, the rabbi scrambled to the window and threw it open: "Come, our widows and orphans are saved!"

The Jews who flocked into the room found neither the sick beggar nor the linen pouch nor the bank notes. The beggar's visit had left behind only a rumpled bed and two cracked window panes.

Satan was baffled. This time the devil had bribed the rabbi privately, with no risk of exposure—but plainly a craving for wealth was not the rabbi's weakness.

The devils were silent, spent. Then Lilith stepped forward and said, "Leave him to me. The old ways are better than the clever. . . ."

Not feeling well, the rabbi sent the beadle for the barber, hoping for relief through a bit of bloodletting. The barber finished just before sunset, and the rabbi had stationed himself at the eastern wall for the prayer of the Eighteen Benedictions when a young woman came in, an unplucked chicken under her arm.

The rabbi prayed; the young woman strolled about the room, humming absently. Her voice was sweet to the ear, but failed to distract the rabbi. Tired, she slumped into a chair and began to rock. The rabbi, who would not yield a moment of grace to the fangs of a snake, endured the creaking and scraping.

The rabbi finished the Benedictions, spat ritually on idolatry, took three steps back, and sat at the bare table. Softly he said, "Tell me about your chicken."

The young woman rose and approached with the fowl, but the rabbi lifted his hand: "Dear child, a Jewish daughter should know how close to come to a man. Put it on the table."

Dropping the chicken, the young woman circled the room restlessly. The hen she had bought from a peasant. Before she could take it to the slaughterer, it escaped. For hours, she had prowled the streets, tracking her chicken. . . .

Her carriage was engaging, her tone gentle. When she laughed her even teeth set off the luster of her eyes. Her dress was short, her sleeves rolled up, and traces of spice cloaked her body. As the rabbi examined the chicken, she placed herself behind him, touching his arm, her breath currying his cheek.

The rabbi held up the chicken and said, "Kosher!" And without turning, he added, "And you, young lady, should find yourself a husband."

The young woman and her chicken soared through the open window.

The rabbi smiled knowingly.

Once again Satan summoned his devils. For every notion there was a snag. A young devil, untested, without a single feather in his cap or tooth on his neck-strand, asked, "Is there nothing this rabbi covets?"

"He's shed desire."

"What does he enjoy?"

"A hot bath on Friday. . . ."

The youthful devil brooded a moment, then said, "He must have habits, such as rolling bread pills after a meal——"

"Unlikely. We've never caught him eating."

Idly, Lilith recalled that the rabbi did have a snuffbox. When her fragrance had reached his nostrils, he had taken a pinch.

"That's it!" the devil shouted, and without begging leave, vanished.

Every Friday, after his bath, the rabbi left Chelm and strolled along a path—between a wheat field and a corn field—reciting the Song of Songs. Easily absorbed, and fearing he might wander too far and violate the Sabbath by returning late, the rabbi had paced off a mark. When he reached his sapling, he would be halfway through the verses, with time to sit a moment, treat himself to an ample pinch of snuff, and finish the second half of the Song on his way back.

Early this Friday, a German turned up—dressed in green-striped trousers and a derby—tore out the tree and carried it farther along the path. Lanky, the German was too thin to be seen when he posted himself behind the replanted trunk.

When the rabbi came to ". . . drink abundantly, O beloved," he was short of his mark. Stung, certain that he had skimmed the verses without thought or feeling, the rabbi, as penance, forfeited his pinch of snuff until he reached the tree.

Weary and footsore, the rabbi limped to the sapling and sagged to the ground. His nostrils burning for the soothing tot of tobacco, his hands trembling, the rabbi opened the birch snuffbox. A gust of wind surged over his shoulder and wrested the box from his fingers. The rabbi reached for the box; another puff rolled it away. The rabbi lunged. The box whirled. On hands and knees—gasping for his pinch of snuff—the rabbi stalked the elusive birch box.

Behind the tree, the German stopped blowing long enough to snicker. Letting loose a final draught of air, the German plucked up and planted the sapling where it had stood originally.

The rabbi looked up, puzzled. Had he drifted that far from his tree? Was it evening?

The sun had set. The stars were out. For a pinch of snuff he had profaned the Sabbath.

Still, the snuffbox lay close beside him. The rabbi pounced; the box tumbled away. . . .

The youthful devil, who had set out without a feather in his cap or a tooth on his neck-strand, waited for the ovation to let up. Then he said, "They're on guard against temptations that rage, but unprepared for the strength of quiet needs. . . ."

And he left on his next mission.

Translated by Reuben Bercovitch

Motl Prince

There was once a Jew whose name was Motl. But he was called Motl Prince.

He dealt in timber and grain. He had free entry to the homes of the nobility, so he acted a bit like an aristocrat himself. He wore silk stockings. He painted the chairs in his house red—no other paint was available in town—and a dainty red handkerchief peeked out of his pocket. Even his charity he dispensed in a lordly manner.

Now, it is known that Jews love goose. First, because it is good to eat, and second, because it is economical—there is the meat, and goose fat for Passover, and cracklings to eat with an onion. Feathers for a pillow are also useful. To this day, when a Jew goes to a restaurant he asks for a listing of the entire menu and in the end orders a piece of goose.

It happened, however, that the rabbi of this town loved ducks. A God-fearing scholar but with a weakness for duck meat. People talked about it, and it reached Motl Prince.

It was before Purim and Motl Prince ordered a duck to be bought and fattened as a Purim gift for the rabbi. And he further ordered that, when it came to stuffing the duck after it had been made properly kosher, he should be informed.

On the eve of Purim he was informed: the time has come to stuff the duck.

Motl Prince took eighteen golden Polish zlotys out of his dresser, ordered that they be made kosher by washing them in seven waters, and that the duck be stuffed with them.

Why?

Motl Prince wanted to know which the rabbi liked more, duck or Polish zlotys.

Once Motl went strolling down the synagogue alley. It was the eve of the Sabbath, on a summer day, and from time to time he took out his dainty red handkerchief, ostensibly to wipe the perspiration from his brow. Each time he pulled out the handkerchief he let slip a *roulon* to the ground.

What is a *roulon*?

At that time there was no paper money in circulation, no credit bills. What was used in trade were gold coins. Merchants would pack the gold coins into paper tubes, seal them with their seals, and write the sum on the tubes. It was these tubes, called *roulons*, that circulated from hand to hand without the contents being counted. There was a bit more trust and confidence then.

Motl strolled along and let slip such *roulons*.

How come?

He took old Polish pennies and packed them into the tubes as if they were gold coins.

Poor people walking in the street would find them. If the finder was honest, he would run after him and return the find, and Motl Prince would reward him with gracious thanks and a gold coin for returning the loss. If the finder was not an honest man, he would grab his find, conceal it, and happily run home with it—but all he would end up with would be a few pennies.

Once on the eve of Passover he played this trick. Since he was *parnas,* the communal provider, he sat in the community house and distributed *ma'ot hittin,* wheat money. Poor Jews came in rags and in tatters, and he would remark to one and then another, "You stingy fellow, will you at least indulge yourself and order some new clothes for the holiday?"

The paupers laughed.

On the eve of *Shabbat Hagadol,* the great Sabbath before Passover, poor people left the bathhouse late—they had to wait till the *ba'ale batim,* the solid citizens, had their turn first. When they came to the cooling room where they had left their clothes—not a trace. Outcries, shouting. Who stole the clothes? How would they get home? They blamed the bathhouse attendant. Motl Prince came in, pretending to have been delayed. He ruled: the paupers were right. The bathhouse attendant was paid for his work and so he must pay.

Well, since Motl Prince so ruled, the attendant went into the adjoining house and returned with a heap of clothes, fresh from the needle, nothing missing, and proceeded to dress and shod the naked ones.

In mid-winter, after a snow had freshly fallen, he plays a trick like this.

In the same synagogue alley, poor people wake early in their little houses; they barely scramble out from amid the rags in which they had wrapped themselves, they pour water on their finger tips, dress, and want to go to early prayer and then to market to earn whatever the good God would provide. But the doors don't open. They must be blocked from outside, sealed, for the frost is sharp. They try the doors again but they do not yield. Terror seizes them. They yell; the men shout, the women shout, the children wail. All of those in the synagogue alley shout. The cry is heard in other streets; people jump out of their beds, they run out of their houses, they come to the synagogue alley, and . . .

Before every door is piled a load of wood.

Motl Prince had ordered the wood brought from the forest during the night. The snowfall had been heavy and nobody heard a sound.

Once Motl Prince came home weary from the forest, lay down to rest before his meal, and dozed off thinking what new charity joke he could play. The door opens and two attendants of the Burial and Pallbearers Society enter and declare: "Motl Prince, be informed that you have passed away."

He answers calmly, "Blessed be the True Judge."

Should anyone speculate who is best prepared for paradise, he would be told by all: Motl Prince.

What has a man like him to fear?

They approach him, take some straw from their pockets and spread it; they raise him up, light a candle at his head, and walk out.

One says he is going to buy cerements. The other, that he is going at once to order a tombstone. On it would be engraved "Motl Prince," nothing more.

Motl Prince thinks to himself: it's quite enough.

He wants to consider why he doesn't see anyone from his household, he wants to recall whether he had said farewell to them, whether or not he had recited the confession—but two strange figures come in; they are not angels, they are not people, they are not beasts. They have thin wings, like bats, and they ask him whether he wants to go to paradise at once.

He forgets about everything else and smiles, "Why not?"

They lift him and hoist him through the chimney to the roof.

He knows that the chimney had not been cleaned in a long time, and he comes out black, asking, "What have I done to deserve this?"

They answer, "One doesn't get to paradise without first being blackened."

Well, if that is the rule!

"Now," they say, "we will fly up, we on our wings, but what will you fly on?"

There appears before him on the roof the broom which stands on his porch and which poor people coming to visit him use for brushing their boots. They say to him, "Get on it."

The broom is not clean. Well, one has to go through with it.

"Such is the custom," they tell him. "As long as the soul still doesn't have its own wings, it rides on a broom."

They hold him between them and fly off.

"Will we be flying long?"

"It's a long way to heaven yet," they tell him.

He understands. It takes time. So they fly on.

He asks, "What time of the year is it?"

They say, "The eve of Sukkoth." And they ask if he wants to sit in a *sukkah*.

It's true that the dead are relieved of all commandments; still, why not sit in a *sukkah*? "Very well," he says. And as he speaks there floats toward them a *sukkah* with walls and a roof of branches.

"This is King David's *sukkah*," they say.

He goes in gaily and sits down. "Will the divine visitors come?" he asks.

But before they answer, the *sukkah* collapses over him and he is barely dragged out, beat up and battered, covered with white dust on top of the black soot from the chimney.

"What have I done to deserve this?" he asks.

"There is no other way to get to paradise than beat up and battered," they tell him.

He submits humbly and they fly on. Then they stop.

"Are we there?" But he sees nothing.

They tell him that though he sees nothing they are already near paradise and it is therefore necessary to blindfold him.

"What for?"

Every saint is entitled to see his own chamber only, they

explain to him. Only later, when other saints come to visit and invite him to their chambers is it possible to see paradise. Since it will be necessary to pass through the chambers of other saints, they must blindfold him.

He submits. They take his dainty, red handkerchief, blindfold him, and fly on. Then they stop again.

"You are already in your chamber."

"Please," he begs, "remove the blindfold."

"Right away." First they must get everything in readiness. First he must change his clothes.

They rip off his old clothes and dress him in others and say, "These are royal garments." They even rip the new clothes, but that is probably the way it has to be.

They set him down and say, "This is your golden throne."

They shove something under his feet. "This is your foot-stool."

They put something on his head. "This is your golden crown."

They shove something in front of him. "This is your table set with the Leviathan and the preserved wine."

And suddenly there is laughter from all sides, and what laughter! Apparently they are in stitches from laughter.

He rips off the blindfold and sees before him a wooden kitchen table, and on it tin plates, like those in a poor house, with black vermin dipped in tar.

His clothes are of pig bristles and they itch. On his head an old sleeping cap, under his feet a cold fire pot, and he sits on a stool with a hole in the center.

Motl awakes from his dream and sees the rabbi sitting at the head of his bed. He had come to ask for a donation and waited for Motl to wake up.

He relates to him the dream just as it was. "Rabbi," he sighs, "why?"

The rabbi lowers his long brows, thinks a while, and answers with a smile: "What did you expect, Motl? When one gives charity as a joke, paradise becomes a mockery."

From that time on Motl gave charity only in secret. In time people began to call him simply Motl. The name "Prince" was forgotten.

Translated by Shlomo Katz

Bontsha the Silent

Here on earth the death of Bontsha the Silent made no impression at all. Ask anyone: Who was Bontsha, how did he live, and how did he die? Did his strength slowly fade, did his heart slowly give out—or did the very marrow of his bones melt under the weight of his burdens? Who knows? Perhaps he just died from not eating—starvation, it's called.

If a horse, dragging a cart through the streets, should fall, people would run from blocks around to stare, newspapers would write about this fascinating event, a monument would be put up to mark the very spot where the horse had fallen. Had the horse belonged to a race as numerous as that of human beings, he wouldn't have been paid this honor. How many horses are there, after all? But human beings—there must be a thousand million of them!

Bontsha was a human being; he lived unknown, in silence, and in silence he died. He passed through our world like a shadow. When Bontsha was born no one took a drink of wine; there was no sound of glasses clinking. When he was confirmed, he made no speech of celebration. He existed like a grain of sand at the rim of a vast ocean, amid millions of other grains of sand exactly similar, and when the wind at last lifted him up and carried him across to the other shore of that ocean, no one noticed, no one at all.

During his lifetime his feet left no mark upon the dust of the streets; after his death the wind blew away the board that marked his grave. The wife of the gravedigger came upon that bit of wood, lying far off from the grave, and she picked it up and used it to make a fire under the potatoes she was cooking; it was just right. Three days after Bontsha's death no one knew where he lay, neither the gravedigger nor anyone else. If Bontsha had had a headstone, someone, even after a hundred years, might have come across it, might still have been able to read the carved words, and his name, Bontsha the Silent, might not have vanished from this earth.

His likeness remained in no one's memory, in no one's heart. A shadow! Nothing! Finished!

In loneliness he lived, and in loneliness he died. Had it not been for the infernal human racket someone or other might have heard the sound of Bontsha's bones cracking under the weight of his burdens; someone might have glanced around and seen that Bontsha was also a human being, that he had two frightened eyes and a silent trembling mouth; someone might have noticed how, even when he bore no actual load upon his back, he still walked with his head bowed down to earth, as though while living he was already searching for his grave.

When Bontsha was brought to the hospital ten people were waiting for him to die and leave them his narrow little cot; when he was brought from the hospital to the morgue twenty were waiting to occupy his pall; when he was taken out of the morgue forty were waiting to lie where he would lie forever. Who knows how many are now waiting to snatch from him that bit of earth?

In silence he was born, in silence he lived, in silence he died—and in an even vaster silence he was put into the ground.

Ah, but in the other world it was not so! No! In paradise the death of Bontsha was an overwhelming event. The great trumpet of the Messiah announced through the seven heavens: Bontsha the Silent is dead! The most exalted angels, with the most imposing wings, hurried, flew, to tell one another, "Do you know who has died? Bontsha! Bontsha the Silent!"

And the new, the young little angels with brilliant eyes, with golden wings and silver shoes, ran to greet Bontsha, laughing in their joy. The sound of their wings, the sound of their silver shoes, as they ran to meet him, and the bubbling of their laughter, filled all paradise with jubilation, and God Himself knew that Bontsha the Silent was at last here.

In the great gateway to heaven Abraham our Father stretched out his arms in welcome and benediction: "Peace be with you!" And on his old face a deep sweet smile appeared.

What, exactly, was going on up there in paradise?

There, in paradise, two angels came bearing a golden throne for Bontsha to sit upon, and for his head a golden crown with glittering jewels.

"But why the throne, the crown, already?" two important

saints asked. "He hasn't even been tried before the heavenly court of justice to which each new arrival must submit." Their voices were touched with envy. "What's going on here, anyway?"

And the angels answered the two important saints that, yes, Bontsha's trial hadn't started yet, but it would only be a formality, even the prosecutor wouldn't dare open his mouth. Why, the whole thing wouldn't take five minutes!

"What's the matter with you?" the angels asked. "Don't you know whom you're dealing with? You're dealing with Bontsha, Bontsha the Silent!"

When the young, the singing angels encircled Bontsha in love, when Abraham our Father embraced him again and again, as a very old friend, when Bontsha heard that a throne waited for him, and for his head a crown, and that when he would stand trial in the court of heaven no one would say a word against him—when he heard all this, Bontsha, exactly as in the other world, was silent. He was silent with fear. His heart shook, in his veins ran ice, and he knew this must all be a dream or simply a mistake.

He was used to both, to dreams and mistakes. How often, in that other world, had he not dreamed that he was wildly shoveling up money from the street, that whole fortunes lay there on the street beneath his hands—and then he would wake and find himself a beggar again, more miserable than before the dream.

How often in that other world had someone smiled at him, said a pleasant word—and then, passing and turning back for another look, had seen his mistake and spat at Bontsha.

Wouldn't that be just my luck, he thought now, and he was afraid to lift his eyes, lest the dream end, lest he awake and find himself again on earth, lying somewhere in a pit of snakes and loathsome vipers, and he was afraid to make the smallest sound, to move so much as an eyelash; he trembled and he could not hear the paeans of the angels; he could not see them as they danced in stately celebration about him; he could not answer the loving greeting of Abraham our Father, "Peace be with you!" And when at last he was led into the great court of justice in paradise he couldn't even say "Good morning." He was paralyzed with fear.

And when his shrinking eyes beheld the floor of the courtroom of justice, his fear, if possible, increased. The floor was of

purest alabaster, embedded with glittering diamonds. On such a
floor stand my feet, thought Bontsha. My feet! He was beside
himself with fear. Who knows, he thought, for what very rich
man, or great learned rabbi, or even saint, this whole thing's
meant? The rich man will arrive, and then it will all be over. He
lowered his eyes; he closed them.

In his fear he did not hear when his name was called out in the
pure angelic voice: "Bontsha the Silent!" Through the ringing in
his ears he could make out no words, only the sound of that voice
like the sound of music, of a violin.

Yet did he, perhaps, after all, catch the sound of his own
name, "Bontsha the Silent?" And then the voice added, "To him
that name is as becoming as a frock coat to a rich man."

What's that? What's he saying? Bontsha wondered, and then
he heard an impatient voice interrupting the speech of his defending angel. "Rich man! Frock coat! No metaphors, please!
And no sarcasm!"

"He never," began the defending angel again, "complained,
not against God, not against man; his eye never grew red with
hatred, he never raised a protest against heaven."

Bontsha couldn't understand a word, and the harsh voice of
the prosecuting angel broke in once more. "Never mind the
rhetoric, please!"

"His sufferings were unspeakable. Here, look upon a man
who was more tormented than Job!"

Who? Bontsha wondered. Who is this man?

"Facts! Facts! Never mind the flowery business and stick to
the facts, please!" the judge called out.

"When he was eight days old he was circumcised——"

"Such realistic details are unnecessary——"

"The knife slipped, and he did not even try to staunch the
flow of blood——"

"——are distasteful. Simply give us the important facts."

"Even then, an infant, he was silent, he did not cry out his
pain," Bontsha's defender continued. "He kept his silence, even
when his mother died, and he was handed over, a boy of thir-
teen, to a snake, a viper—a stepmother!"

Hm, Bontsha thought, could they mean me?

"She begrudged him every bite of food, even the moldy rotten
bread and the gristle of meat that she threw at him, while she
herself drank coffee with cream."

"Irrelevant and immaterial," said the judge.

"For all that, she didn't begrudge him her pointed nails in his flesh—flesh that showed black and blue through the rags he wore. In winter, in the bitterest cold, she made him chop wood in the yard, barefoot! More than once were his feet frozen, and his hands, that were too young, too tender, to lift the heavy logs and chop them. But he was always silent, he never complained, not even to his father——"

"Complain! To that drunkard!" The voice of the prosecuting angel rose derisively, and Bontsha's body grew cold with the memory of fear.

"He never complained," the defender continued, "and he was always lonely. He never had a friend, never was sent to school, never was given a new suit of clothes, never knew one moment of freedom."

"Objection! Objection!" the prosecutor cried out angrily. "He's only trying to appeal to the emotions with these flights of rhetoric!"

"He was silent even when his father, raving drunk, dragged him out of the house by the hair and flung him into the winter night, into the snowy, frozen night. He picked himself up quietly from the snow and wandered into the distance where his eyes led him.

"During his wanderings he was always silent; during his agony of hunger he begged only with his eyes. And at last, on a damp spring night, he drifted to a great city, drifted there like a leaf before the wind, and on his very first night, scarcely seen, scarcely heard, he was thrown into jail. He remained silent, he never protested, he never asked, Why, what for? The doors of the jail were opened again, and, free, he looked for the most lowly filthy work, and still he remained silent.

"More terrible even than the work itself was the search for work. Tormented and ground down by pain, by the cramp of pain in an empty stomach, he never protested, he always kept silent.

"Soiled by the filth of a strange city, spat upon by unknown mouths, driven from the streets into the roadway, where, a human beast of burden, he pursued his work, a porter, carrying the heaviest loads upon his back, scurrying between carriages, carts, and horses, staring death in the eyes every moment, he still kept silent.

"He never reckoned up how many pounds he must haul to earn a penny; how many times, with each step, he stumbled and fell for that penny. He never reckoned up how many times he almost vomited out his very soul, begging for his earnings. He never reckoned up his bad luck, the other's good luck. No, never. He remained silent. He never even demanded his own earnings; like a beggar, he waited at the door for what was rightfully his, and only in the depths of his eyes was there an unspoken longing. 'Come back later!' they'd order him; and, like a shadow, he would vanish, and then, like a shadow, would return and stand waiting, his eyes begging, imploring, for what was his. He remained silent even when they cheated him, keeping back, with one excuse or another, most of his earnings, or giving him bad money. Yes, he never protested, he always remained silent.

"Once," the defending angel went on, "Bontsha crossed the roadway to the fountain for a drink, and in that moment his whole life was miraculously changed. What miracle happened to change his whole life? A splendid coach, with tires of rubber, plunged past, dragged by runaway horses; the coachman, fallen, lay in the street, his head split open. From the mouths of the frightened horses spilled foam, and in their wild eyes sparks struck like fire in a dark night, and inside the carriage sat a man, half alive, half dead, and Bontsha caught at the reins and held the horses. The man who sat inside and whose life was saved, a Jew, a philanthropist, never forgot what Bontsha had done for him. He handed him the whip of the dead driver, and Bontsha, then and there, became a coachman—no longer a common porter! And what's more, his great benefactor married him off, and what's still more, this great philanthropist himself provided a child for Bontsha to look after.

"And still Bontsha never said a word, never protested."

They mean me, I really do believe they mean me, Bontsha encouraged himself, but still he didn't have the gall to open his eyes, to look up at his judge.

"He never protested. He remained silent even when that great philanthropist shortly thereafter went into bankruptcy without ever having paid Bontsha one cent of his wages.

"He was silent even when his wife ran off and left him with her helpless infant. He was silent when, fifteen years later, that same helpless infant had grown up and become strong enough to throw Bontsha out of the house."

They mean me, Bontsha rejoiced, they really mean me.

"He even remained silent," continued the defending angel, "when that same benefactor and philanthropist went out of bankruptcy, as suddenly as he'd gone into it, and still didn't pay Bontsha one cent of what he owed him. No, more than that. This person, as befits a fine gentleman who has gone through bankruptcy, again went driving the great coach with the tires of rubber, and now, now he had a new coachman, and Bontsha, again a porter in the roadway, was run over by coachman, carriage, horses. And still, in his agony, Bontsha did not cry out; he remained silent. He did not even tell the police who had done this to him. Even in the hospital, where everyone is allowed to scream, he remained silent. He lay in utter loneliness on his cot, abandoned by the doctor, by the nurse; he had not the few pennies to pay them—and he made no murmur. He was silent in that awful moment just before he was about to die, and he was silent in that very moment when he did die. And never one murmur of protest against man, never one murmur of protest against God!"

Now Bontsha begins to tremble again. He senses that after his defender has finished, his prosecutor will rise to state the case against him. Who knows of what he will be accused? Bontsha, in that other world on earth, forgot each present moment as it slipped behind him to become the past. Now the defending angel has brought everything back to his mind again—but who knows what forgotten sins the prosecutor will bring to mind?

The prosecutor rises. "Gentlemen!" he begins in a harsh and bitter voice, and then he stops. "Gentlemen——" he begins again, and now his voice is less harsh, and again he stops. And finally, in a very soft voice, that same prosecutor says, "Gentlemen, he was always silent—and now I too will be silent."

The great court of justice grows very still, and at last from the judge's chair a new voice rises, loving, tender. "Bontsha my child, Bontsha"—the voice swells like a great harp—"my heart's child . . ."

Within Bontsha his very soul begins to weep. He would like to open his eyes, to raise them, but they are darkened with tears. It is so sweet to cry. Never until now has it been sweet to cry.

"My child, my Bontsha . . ."

Not since his mother died has he heard such words, and spoken in such a voice.

"My child," the judge begins again, "you have always suffered, and you have always kept silent. There isn't one secret place in your body without its bleeding wound; there isn't one secret place in your soul without its wound and blood. And you never protested. You always were silent.

"There, in that other world, no one understood you. You never understood yourself. You never understood that you need not have been silent, that you could have cried out and that your outcries would have brought down the world itself and ended it. You never understood your sleeping strength. There in that other world, that world of lies, your silence was never rewarded, but here in paradise is the world of truth, here in paradise you will be rewarded. You, the judge can neither condemn nor pass sentence upon. For you there is not only one little portion of paradise, one little share. No, for you there is everything! Whatever you want! Everything is yours!"

Now for the first time Bontsha lifts his eyes. He is blinded by light. The splendor of light lies everywhere, upon the walls, upon the vast ceiling, the angels blaze with light, the judge. He drops his weary eyes.

"Really?" he asks, doubtful, and a little embarrassed.

"Really!" the judge answers. "Really! I tell you, everything is yours. Everything in paradise is yours. Choose! Take! Whatever you want! You will only take what is yours!"

"Really?" Bontsha asks again, and now his voice is stronger, more assured.

And the judge and all the heavenly host answer, "Really! Really! Really!"

"Well then"—and Bontsha smiles for the first time—"well then, what I would like, Your Excellency, is to have, every morning for breakfast, a hot roll with fresh butter."

A silence falls upon the great hall, and it is more terrible than Bontsha's has ever been, and slowly the judge and the angels bend their heads in shame at this unending meekness they have created on earth.

Then the silence is shattered. The prosecutor laughs aloud, a bitter laugh.

Translated by Hilde Abel

Joy Beyond Measure

As is well known, our sort of Hasidim have always observed Rosh Hashanah as an occasion for gaiety.

After all, we are not *misnagdim*. We don't tremble in terror of the judgment day.

For we know that we will not stand before a strange ruler, that a father will judge us. So we take a drop of liquor and after the prayers we dance a bit.

But one time we had a Rosh Hashanah that exceeded all other Rosh Hashanahs.

It began as usual. But on the very first day a conflagration broke out.

Our rabbi, the Old One, does not let anyone else be cantor during the Days of Awe. He does not depend on anyone.

So he served as cantor.

And how he prays—this I don't have to tell you.

When in the prayers he reached "To God who decrees Law," he shouted out its words in his melodious voice: *L'El orekh din!*

Hearts were made to tremble, the very heavens rent open.

And so on and on: "To Him who probes hearts. . . . To Him who reveals depths . . ."

But when he reached "To Him who sees that which is concealed," his voice broke. It faltered, it was unsure. Its tone changed. "To Him who acquires . . ." sounded weak. "His servants" expressed doubt, and "by law" was despairing.

Then suddenly he fell silent altogether. A minute, two minutes, three, and more. Each minute felt like a year. Terror all around. It was hard to breathe. The women's section appeared to be in a swoon—not a sound from there.

Suddenly he stirred. A tremor passed through his entire body, and the terrified and awed silence was broken by a joyous:

"To Him who is merciful to His people on judgment day," which he long and gaily trilled. His very bones sang. His feet danced, right there by the cantor's stand. And so it continued till he finished the morning prayers. As if he had found new powers!

And then the Old One told us what had happened. It was quite something.

When one prays out of a prayer book, the eyes run ahead of the lips. When the Old One intoned "To Him who sees . . ." his eyes already read "To Him who acquires." And when this happened, everything became confused and he didn't seem to understand the meaning of the words he was saying. For, really, who acquires servants in judgment?

Having no answer, he was confused and fell silent.

But up in heaven they did not want to allow that the Old One's prayers should become garbled and they showed him what it all meant. As soon as he closed his eyes to think the matter over, the heavens opened and he beheld—the courtroom, the heavenly courtroom, the true place of judgment. Here was the table, and here the scales of justice.

It must have been early because no one was there. So he looked around. Five doors opened into the courtroom. Two at the sides, right and left. Over the door on the right it said Defense, and over the door on the left Prosecution. Three doors opened from the rear wall, the east wall, behind the table and the scales of justice. The middle of the three doors was closed; those to its right and left were open. Over the closed door it said Heavenly Court. Through the open doors one could see, on the right, paradise, the patriarchs and saints—lit up by the light of the Holy Spirit—with crowns on their heads, engaged in study. Apparently they have no judgment day.

And through the left door one could see hell. It was quiet and empty in hell. Apparently, on holidays punishment and torture are suspended. The sinners are free, and their tormentors occupied elsewhere. Just where they are occupied you will learn later in this story. But the fire in hell continued to burn. As it says in Scriptures: "And the fire shall never be extinguished."

The door to the right opened and the defense counsel came in carrying a bundle of good deeds under his arm. A little bundle. It had not been much of a year for good deeds. Seeing that the door to the left was still closed, he understood that the prosecution was still busy collecting its documents. It must have been a good year for the prosecution. The defense counsel put his bundle down and mournfully seated himself.

Then the door on the left opened and two devils entered bowed under the burden of a heavy load. Their very bones crackled under the weight. They threw it down, caught their breath, and as they walked out they said to the defense attorney, "This isn't even a tenth of what we have. Others will bring more. Little devils are collecting it. There are entire treasures of it."

The defense attorney was saddened. He covered his face and sighed.

He thought nobody heard him. The heavenly court was still out. In paradise all were busy with their studies. Hell was empty.

But among those in paradise there was Rabbi Levi-Yitzkhok of Berdichev—and he heard.

He alone remembered that among the dwellers of darkness in the shadow of death in the valley of murk below, today was judgment day. And if someone in heaven sighed, it must be in connection with them. So he paused in his studies and looked about himself.

And he saw who it was that sighed—the defense attorney in the courtroom.

In that case, he had to find out what it was all about.

Without further ado Levi-Yitzkhok interrupted his studies, rose and tiptoed out of paradise into the courtroom, and there saw the little bundle of good deeds and the big load of sins. Now he grasped how matters stood. Without thinking overlong, he picked up the load of sins and flung it through the open door on the left into the fire of hell, where it was at once consumed.

Now came two other devils, again carrying a load. They went out and Rabbi Levi-Yitzkhok again grabbed the load and tossed it into the flames where it burned, was consumed, and was no more.

The same with the third, the fourth, and all the rest of the loads of sins. As soon as the devils go out, the load goes flying into the fire.

Finally, as the last load is still burning, Satan himself comes in, with leisurely step, happy and gay. But he sees no sign of his treasures. He looks about, sees what is burning and notices Levi-Yitzkhok about to walk back to paradise. He is no fool, Satan isn't, and he understands at once what had happened. He grabs

Levi-Yitzkhok by the arm and shouts at the top of his voice, "Thief!"

People come running from paradise. The middle door opens and the heavenly court enters. The defense attorney uncovers his face and jumps up.

"What's going on?"

Satan the destroyer tells what happened. He had caught Levi-Yitzkhok red-handed. The last sack of sins, the heaviest one, was still burning.

He obviously was telling the truth. Nor did Levi-Yitzkhok deny it.

They ask Satan what he wants, what kind of verdict.

He does not take long to answer. He wants everything according to law. It is written that a thief should be sold for his theft. Well then, let Levi-Yitzkhok be sold for a slave, right then and there, publicly, in the courtroom. Whoever wants to can bid for him. He, Satan himself, also wants to bid. He will make sure to recoup his loss.

And the heavenly court has to admit that he is right. There must be an auction—and Levi-Yitzkhok will not be lost, they figure. Heaven won't permit it.

The two parties form at the scales of justice; the destroyer on one side and all the denizens of paradise on the other.

Levi-Yitzkhok stands in the middle, as if it doesn't concern him at all.

Ransom is being tossed into the scales, from the right and the left, each outdoing the other.

The heavenly court sits at the table and watches.

Father Abraham steps up and throws his first *mitzvah* into the scale, adding to it his hospitality. After him Isaac throws in having been offered as a sacrifice. Jacob adds his innocence and the fact that he dwelt in his tent and devoted himself to study while Esau was out in the forest hunting. After Jacob, Rachel tosses in her love-mandrakes. The other matriarchs follow, and then the saints toss in their treasures to the acclaim of all.

But Satan has uncounted and unimagined treasures in his kingdom. After every addition from the right he throws in something from the left and his side of the scales keeps descending. He tosses in treasure after treasure—from under the earth, from beyond the mountains of darkness, from all the secret places of his kingdom. Treasures—such as no eye ever beheld before. He is determined. He must have Levi-Yitzkhok. He wants him as a stoker of fires in hell. And finally he pulls the crown from off his head and throws it into the scale which trembles a moment, then goes down, down, down.

Things look bad.

Last comes the defense attorney and throws in the small bundle of good deeds on his side of the scale but it makes hardly any impression. The tongue of the scale does not budge.

The destroyer's face becomes distorted with a triumphant grin and his eyes flare with victory. He places his right hand on Levi-Yitzkhok's shoulder and with his left hand directs him to the door of hell.

There is turmoil. Levi-Yitzkhok is lost. Commotion! Confusion! What should be done? What?

The noise mounts and is suddenly rent in two. A voice from on high, from the throne of glory: "I buy him!"

Silence. And the Lord of the Universe declares: "I offer more. 'For the whole world is mine.' I offer the world for Rabbi Levi-Yitzkhok."

The destroyer's face turned black.

This is what the Old One told us. You can imagine what kind of prayers we had and what kind of Rosh Hashanah we had. The case of the prosecution burnt. A signed and sealed decree for a good year to come practically in our pockets. Levi-Yitzkhok ransomed. The mystery of the incomprehensible "To Him who acquires His servants by law" revealed.

There was joy beyond measure.

Translated by Shlomo Katz

Between Two Peaks *

You have surely heard of the Brisker Rov and of the Bialer Rebbe. But it is not generally known that the rebbe of Biala had once been a favorite pupil of the other. He had studied in the rov's yeshivah for a number of years, only to disappear and lead the life of a penniless wanderer until the day he was "revealed" in Biala.

He had left the rov's yeshivah for the following reason. They were studying the Torah, but he felt the kind of Torah that they studied was lifeless. Here is a regulation that concerns the cleanliness of females; a law relating to money; a question on the subject of meat and milk. These are real. A female wants a ruling. A servant comes to make an inquiry. Simon and Reuben come to have a lawsuit. In such a moment, the studies come alive. They acquire strength, a dominion in the world. But when this did not happen, when the problems were irrelevant, the rebbe felt that the studies were arid. This is the surface. It is the body, not the spirit of the Torah. Torah has to live!

Kabbalistic books were forbidden in the town of Brisk. The rov was a *misnagid*, a foe of the Hasidim. By nature, he was quick to anger and vindictive as a serpent. If someone merely touched a Zohar, the rov would declare him cursed, putting a decree of anathema upon him. Once, when a Hasid was caught with a forbidden volume, he had his beard shaven off by Gentiles. The victim lost his senses; he fell into a depression. And, surprisingly enough, no hasidic rebbe could help him. (You do not trifle with

---

*This story, one of the major works in the Peretz canon, requires from the reader at least an awareness of the bitter struggle which raged in East European Jewish life during the eighteenth and nineteenth centuries between the sects of Hasidism, or religious enthusiasts, and their rationalist-orthodox opponents, or *misnagdim*. In the story, the term "rov" is used for a rabbi of the latter persuasion, while the term "rebbe" is used for a rabbi or spokesman of the Hasidim.

someone like the Brisker Rov.) Yet—the rebbe wondered—how could he bring himself to leave the Brisker Rov's yeshivah?

For a long time, he wrestled with his problem.

Then a dream was sent to show him the answer. He dreamed the rov came to see him and said, "Come, Noah, I will lead you to the human paradise." He took the rebbe's hand, and he led him into a large palace that had no windows and no door except the one by which they had entered. In spite of this, the room was bright. Because—or so it seemed to the rebbe in his dream—the walls were made of crystal and they gave off their own glittering light.

They kept walking, but they saw no end.

"Hold on to my coat," said the Brisker Rov. "These rooms are beyond all telling, beyond all count. If you do not hold on to me, you will be wandering forever."

The rebbe did as he was told. He continued to walk, but wherever he looked, he saw no bench, no chair, no piece of furniture. Nothing.

"This is not meant for sitting," the Brisker Rov explained. "One just goes on. Farther and farther." So the rebbe follows. Each of the halls is larger and more radiant than the one before it. And the walls are shining—here with one color, there with another; here with a few, there with all colors. Yet, as they walked, they met no human being.

The rebbe grew tired. He was covered with a cold sweat. Hands and feet grew cold. His eyes began to hurt because of the increasing glitter.

He was seized by loneliness, a longing for people, for friends, for the people of Israel. It is no joke not to have a single Jew—a human being—near you!

"Do not long for anyone," said the Brisker Rov. "This is a palace just for me and you. Someday, you too will be the Brisker Rov!"

At this, the rebbe grew still more terrified. He leaned against the wall so as not to fall. But the wall burned him. Not like fire, but like ice!

"Master," he cried, "the walls are made of ice. They are not crystal. They are simply ice."

The rov did not answer. Once more, the rebbe cried, "Master, let me out! I don't want to be here with nobody but you. I want to be with the people of Israel."

No sooner did he say this than the rov vanished. Now the rebbe was alone in the palace.

He saw no way to go out or in. A cold fear beat against him from the walls. His yearning to see a human being—if only a shoemaker or a tailor—became stronger and stronger. He began to cry. "Oh, God!" he pleaded, "take me out of this place! Better to be in hell with the people of Israel than here in this palace by myself."

That very moment there appeared before him a Jew, a simple fellow, with the red girdle of a coachman about his hips, a long whip in his hand. Without a word, this man took him by the sleeve and led him out of the palace. Then he disappeared.

This was the dream that was revealed to the rebbe.

When the rebbe awoke, it was early morning. It scarcely had begun to gray. He understood that this was more than an idle dream. The rebbe dressed quickly and hurried to the House of Study to have his dream interpreted by the scholars who spend the night there. But, going through the market, he saw a covered wagon, a harnessed, large, old-fashioned wagon. Beside it stood a driver, a long whip in his hand, a red girdle round his hips, precisely like the fellow who in his dream had led him from the palace.

He knew they were not strangers. So the rebbe walked up to the other and said, "Which way are you going?"

"Not in your direction," the driver answered coarsely.

"Tell me," he pleaded. "Maybe you can take me with you."

The driver thought it over for a couple of moments, and then he answered: "Why can't you go on foot—a young man like you? Go your own way!"

"Where should I go?"

"Where your eyes will lead you. No concern of mine." And the driver turned away.

The rebbe understanding the meaning of this answer, went into his years of exile.

As I have said, he was "revealed" in Biala. (How it happened is a thing I will not tell—though it's an astonishing story.) About a year later, a householder from Biala, Yehiel by name, brought me there to be a tutor to his children.

At first I thought I would not take the post. You should understand that this Yehiel was rich. The old kind of rich man; he was stuffed with money. He would give a thousand gold pieces to each daughter for a dowry. His children married into the best rabbinical families. Indeed, his most recent daughter-in-law was a daughter of the Brisker Rov.

You can see it yourself. The Brisker Rov, and the other in-laws, are opposed to the Hasidim, and Yehiel is of course a soldier in their ranks. I, by contrast, am a disciple of the Bialer Rebbe. How can I allow myself to enter such a hostile house?

Still—I was drawn to Biala. It meant being in the same town as my rebbe. Something to consider. I made a decision: I went.

As it turned out, Yehiel, my employer, was a decent man. I would even swear that, in his heart, he was strongly attracted to the idea of a hasidic rebbe. He was not a learned man; he watched the Brisker Rov with the same awe as a hen looks at a human being. Nor did he forbid me to be a Hasid of the Bialer Rebbe. But he was careful to keep himself aloof. When I told a story about the Bialer Rebbe, he pretended to yawn, though I could see that his ears were straining to listen. As for Yehiel's son, the one who was married to the daughter of the Brisker Rov, he would wrinkle his brow as he looked at me with anger and derision. But he did not argue. By nature, he was a man who didn't say much.

Now it came to pass that this daughter-in-law, the daughter of the Brisker Rov, was about to have a baby. Nothing remarkable in this. A young wife is pregnant. But that isn't the whole story! It was well known that the Brisker Rov, because he had forced a Hasid to shave—that is, he had ordered a Jewish beard and earlocks to be shaved by Gentiles—had fallen into disfavor with the saints of our generation. In a period of five, six years, he had lost both his sons. None of his three daughters had given him a male grandchild. Not to mention that each had a difficult child-birth. It was touch and go.

Everybody knew this was a punishment visited upon the rov. Only he himself, though his eyes were clear, could not see and realize. (Maybe he did not want to.) He continued to oppose us with an iron hand. With excommunication and persecution of decent men—as he had previously done.

To tell the truth, I was sorry for Gittel, as the daughter of the Brisker Rov was called. A pity that she had these troubles. In the first place, she was a human being. In the second, a good human being. Such a saintly creature! I did not know her equal in this world.

Anytime a poor girl got married, she got Gittel's help. Such a precious creature! Why should she be punished for her father's anger? That is why, once I noticed that the grandmother is getting things ready for the confinement, I began to do what I could to persuade them to get in touch with my rebbe. Let them write a letter of request. They won't have to make a payment. The rebbe doesn't need it. He does not believe in payments.

However, to whom can I speak?

I tried Gittel's husband. I knew his soul was entwined in hers. No matter how he might try to conceal it, domestic bliss was visible in every corner, in all their looks and gestures. But he's a son-in-law of the Brisker Rov! Ask a Hasid for help? He spit, went away, and left me standing with my mouth open.

I turned to his father, Yehiel himself. He answered, "She's a daughter of the Brisker Rov. I cannot do this to him! No, not even if—God forbid—it gets to be a matter of life and death!"

So I went to Yehiel's wife. A decent woman, but unlettered. She answered in this fashion: "If my husband tells me, I'll hurry and send my earrings and holiday headpiece to your rebbe. It cost a fortune! But, if he doesn't—not a single penny. Not even a button."

"Just a letter of request—how would that hurt?"

"Only if my husband knows," she answered me, as a decent woman ought to. Then she turned away. I saw that she did it only to conceal her tears. A mother! A heart has its knowledge. She could feel the danger.

On hearing Gittel's first cry, I ran, nonetheless, to the Bialer Rebbe.

"Shmyeh," he said. "What can I do? I will offer prayer!"

"Rebbe," I begged. "Give me something—anything whatever—for the woman in labor. Something to protect her. A coin, an amulet. Something you have blessed."

"It will only make things worse. Such things are harmful if there is no faith, and she doesn't believe."

What could I do? It was in the early days of Sukkoth; she was in labor. But, in Yehiel's house, I had no way to help her. So I thought it better to be with my rebbe. I will be there often. My eyes will look to the rebbe with supplication. I may persuade him to take pity.

Reports were not good. Gittel was in the third day of her pain. They had done all that human beings could do. They implored the synagogue, burning many hundredweights of candles there and in the houses of study. As for charity—they gave away a fortune, beyond measure. All of the clothes closets were left wide open. Coins of every kind lay in a mound upon the table. Poor people came into the house. Anyone could take anything he wanted, in any quantity he wished.

I was touched.

"Rebbe," I said, "is it not written that charity will save from death?"

"Maybe," he said, "the Brisker Rov will come." I thought his words not entirely to the point. But, at that moment, Yehiel came into the room. He did not speak to the rebbe—as if he didn't see him. "Shmyeh," he said to me, taking hold of my lapel. "There is a coach in back. Get in and go to the Brisker Rov. Let him come here." Yehiel knew how serious it was, because he added, "Let him see for himself what the situation is. The rov will tell us what ought to be done."

Yehiel's face—how shall I describe it? A cadaver is more beautiful!

I was on my way.

I was thinking that, if the rebbe knows that the rov is coming, this ought to lead to something. Even reconciliation! Not between the rov and rebbe. They have no quarrel—but between their factions. When the rov arrives, he will see the truth. He has a pair of eyes.

But it seems that Heaven wouldn't let this happen quickly. Heaven fought against me. I was scarcely out of Biala, when a cloud came rushing into the sky. A cloud, black and heavy like tar. And it began to blow as if spirits were flying from all directions at once.

A peasant understands these matters. The driver crosses himself and, pointing his whip to the sky, says it will be a difficult journey. While he's making these predictions, an even more violent wind rips the cloud apart as if tearing a piece of paper and starts to pile the fragments, each upon the other, as if it were driving the ice floes on a lake. I could see two and three layers of this cloud above my head.

I was not afraid in the beginning. It was no novelty for me to get wet. And I did not fear the thunder. In the first place, it does not thunder in the Sukkoth season. In the second, there was the rebbe's blowing of the ram's horn on Yom Kippur. After these notes, his Hasidim took it for granted that thunder would be no danger in the coming year. Yet it suddenly crackled into my face like a whip. Once, twice, a third time. I lost my confidence. I felt the skies had hit me. They were trying to push me back to Biala. And the peasant was also trying to persuade me—"Let us go home!"

But a life was at stake. I was in the wagon, yet, in the middle of the storm, I could hear a young woman wailing in the throes of labor. I saw her husband cracking his knuckles, wringing his hands. I saw before me Yehiel's gloomy face, its sunken, burning eyes. "Drive!" he kept pleading. "Drive"—and we drove!

And it keeps pouring. It streams from above and squirts from under wheels and below the horse's feet. The road is drenched, entirely covered with water, and over the water, a lather of foam.

What is there to add? We lost our way—and yet I was able to continue.

I brought back the rov to Biala on the seventh day of Sukkoth.

To tell the truth, as soon as the rov took his place in the wagon, the world became quiet. The clouds drifted apart, sunlight shone through. And in due course—calmly and all dry—we rode into Biala. Even the driver had noticed the sudden change in weather, saying in Polish, "The old rabbi or the young?"

But it's more important to tell you what happened when we came into Yehiel's house.

The women who were there came swarming to the Brisker Rov like locusts. They almost fell on their faces before him. We could not hear Gittel in the second room. Either because of the weeping of these women; or maybe—God forbid—because she had no strength left for screaming. Yehiel didn't even see us. He was standing with his forehead pressed against a pane of glass.

The rov's son-in-law didn't turn to greet us either. He was facing the wall, his head beating against it; and I could feel his body trembling.

I thought I would faint. That is how their fear and pain affected me. My limbs grew numb. I felt that my spirit was becoming cold.

Did you know the Brisker Rov? A man! A pillar of stone —believe me!

A tall man. Tall! From the shoulders up, like King Saul himself. He stood higher than all others. He threw an atmosphere of majesty around him. A long, white beard, I remember how (it could be happening today) one of its points turned underneath his belt. The other corner of his beard was quivering above it.

His eyebrows—white, thick, and long—they hid half his face, and when he raised them . . . oh, Almighty God! The women fell back, as if a crash of thunder had struck them. He had such eyes! Knife blades, naked blades, flashed within them. With a lion's roar, he cried, "Women! Away!"

Then, softly and gently, he asked, "Where is my daughter?" When they showed him, he went into the other room. I did not follow.

I was in a daze. Such eyes, such a look and voice! This is another world than that of the rebbe, another way of life. The eyes of the rebbe are mild, so kind that they bring delight to your heart. When he looks at you his glance covers you with gold. And the rebbe's voice, sweet and silken—God! It touches your heart. It caresses so joyously, yet softly. . . . You do not fear him. Your spirit melts with love, the deep kindliness of love. It seeks to leave your body and join the rebbe's soul. It leaps like a moth to a pure flame. But here, in the presence of the Brisker Rov—you feel awe and terror. A commanding figure, a giant from the days of old. And to think that somebody like that is striding into the bedroom of a frail woman in labor!

I was frightened. "He will crush her. She will turn into a bag of bones."

I hurried to the rebbe.

But the rebbe was smiling as he met me at the door.

"Have you seen him? The glory of the Torah. The true essence of our Torah."

I became calm.

If the rebbe is smiling, all is going to be well.

And it was. Gittel was delivered on the eve of Simhath Torah. And the next day, as if nothing had happened, the rov was expounding Torah at Yehiel's table. I would have preferred to be sitting at a different board. But I was afraid to leave, especially since I was needed to make up a *minyan*. (We were going to say the prayer of thanksgiving.)

The way he spoke about the Torah! How shall I describe it? If the Torah is an ocean, then the Brisker Rov was the Leviathan within it. With a single phrase, he swam through ten tractates. With a single citation, he was able to encompass the Talmud and its commentaries. Words resounded and surged, simmered and boiled—just as people who have seen it tell you the ocean does. I was overwhelmed. But "the heart knows the bitterness within the soul." I did not feel that this was a true rejoicing, a true Simhath Torah. That is when I remembered the story of my rebbe's dream.

A chill went through me. The sun lay against the window. There was no lack of wine at the table. I could see that everyone was sweating. But I felt cold—as cold as ice. And I knew that, in the other place, the table of the Bialer Rebbe, a different person was expounding a different kind of Torah. There it was light and warm. Every word was steeped, was interwoven, with ecstasy and love. You felt the presence of angels in the room. You could actually hear the whirring of their big, white wings. Oh, God! But there was no way for me to be there.

Suddenly the rov broke off in the middle of his exposition. "What sort of hasidic rebbe do you have in Biala?"

"A certain Noah."

I felt a twinge. To speak of my rebbe as "a certain Noah"—what impiety!

"He is a wonder-worker?" the Brisker Rov continued.

"That is not what we're told. Some women say he is. But nobody believes them."

"He just takes their money? Without any miracle?"

They answered truthfully that he takes little and gives most of it away.

The rov grew thoughtful. "Is he a good scholar?"

"According to reports, he is a great one."

"Where does this Noah come from?"

No one knew. I was forced to answer and a dialogue began between the rov and me.

"Wasn't this Noah at one time in Brisk?"

I began to stammer. "Was the rebbe in Brisk? Yes, I believe he was."

"Oh!" he said. "Here is one of his disciples!" I thought he looked at me the way he would at a spider.

Turning to the others, he said, "I once had a pupil whose name was Noah. Even had a good mind. Only he felt an attraction to the other side. I spoke to him about it—I spoke again. I was about to warn him for the third time, but he disappeared. Is it the same Noah?"

"Who can say?"

So the Brisker Rov started to describe his pupil: short, thin, a little black beard, wavy black earlocks, with a soft voice, thoughtful, easy to approach. And the crowd said, "Yes! It could be. That is very close."

I was glad when it was time for the benediction. The questions had to stop. But, after this was done, a thing happened that I could not have imagined, not even in my dreams.

The rov got up, took me aside, and whispered: "Take me to your teacher, to my pupil. Only—hear me! I want nobody to know."

I obeyed him, of course. As we're walking, I inquired timidly. "Brisker Rov," I said, "what is the reason for your visit?"

And he answered simply, "It struck me, while saying the benediction, that I had decided without having seen him. I want to meet him, to see him for myself." Later he added, "Maybe God will help me, and I will be able to rescue one of my pupils.

"You know, you heathen," he continued with a twinkle, "if your rebbe is the Noah who was once my pupil, he may yet be a great man in Israel. Some day, he may even be a Brisker Rov."

At this point, I lost any doubts I had. I knew that my rebbe was the Noah who had studied in the rov's yeshivah. And my heart began to tremble.

The two peaks met. It's a miracle from heaven I was not crushed between them.

The rebbe of Biala—may his memory be blessed—every Simhath Torah used to send his Hasidim for a walk around the city. He would sit on his porch, look at them, and enjoy it.

This was not the Biala of today. It was a little town. Low, very tiny houses—except for the synagogue and the rebbe's house of study. The rebbe's porch was on the second floor. From it, you could see—as plainly as upon your palm—little hills in the east, the river to the west. From the little porch, the rebbe watches his disciples. If he sees that any group is silent, the rebbe, from on high, throws them the beginning of a tune. His Hasidim pick it up. From that moment on, they keep chanting as they walk. In groups, in groups, they are going by, moving out of town—with song, true joy, true rejoicing of the Torah. The rebbe watches, and he does not stir.

This time, apparently, he heard a different step. My rebbe stood up and welcomed the Brisker Rov.

"*Sholom aleykhem,* teacher." He spoke with deference.

"*Aleykhem sholom,* Noah." the Brisker Rov replied.

"Teacher, please sit."

The Brisker Rov sat down. The rebbe stood before him.

The rov raised his eyebrows. "Tell me, Noah," he said, "why did you run away from the yeshivah? What was it that you didn't find there?"

"Teacher," he answered calmly, "there was no air. I could not catch my breath."

"What do you mean? What are you saying, Noah?"

"Not I," the rebbe quietly explained. "It was my soul that felt a lack of air."

"Why was that, Noah?"

"Because your Torah, teacher, is a matter of rules. It is without compassion. No spark of charity! That is why there is no joy within it. One cannot breathe deeply. Iron laws, regulations of copper. A very lofty Torah; but it's for the scholar, the exceptional person."

The Brisker Rov was silent and the rebbe continued. "Teacher, tell me! What do you have for the people? For the simple craftsman? For a woodchopper or butcher? For the ordinary man? Most of all, for a man who is sinful? Teacher, what do you give to those who are not scholars?"

The Brisker Rov was silent, as if he could not understand what was being said. And the rebbe continued, standing in front of him and speaking in his soft voice.

"Teacher, please forgive me. I must tell the truth. Your Torah was hard—unyielding and dry. It was merely the body, not the spirit of the Law."

"Spirit?" said the Brisker Rov. He rubbed his high forehead.

"Of course! Your Torah, as I've told you, is only for scholars, those who are superior. But the Torah is for all! The Holy Spirit must rest upon all Israel, because in the Torah is Israel's soul."

"And your Torah, Noah?"

"Do you want to see it?"

"See it? Torah?" the Brisker Rov was puzzled.

"Teacher, I will show it to you. Come! I will show its light. The joy that radiates from it, over everybody, over all of Israel."

The rov did not move.

"Teacher, I beg you. Come. It is not far."

The rebbe led the rov out on the little porch. I followed them softly.

Still, my rebbe could feel it. "You may follow, Shmyeh. You will see it this time. The rov will see it, too. . . . You will realize what this holiday means. You will see a true rejoicing of the Torah."

I saw the same as on other Simhath Torahs. But I saw it differently. As if a veil had fallen from my eyes!

A big, wide sky, truly without limit. Blue, pale blue, a delight to see. And, across the sky, the white, almost silver, clouds were floating. And if you watched them closely, you could see how they were shivering as if with joy, dancing in the happiness of their Simhath Torah.

In the background, a broad green belt encircled the town. It was dark, yet the color was alive, as if a living spirit was flying among the grasses. Now and then, you had the impression that—always in a different place—a spirit that was zestful, vital, broke out into flame. You would sense how little fires were leaping, dancing among the grasses, touching them, caressing.

On the meadows with their sparkle, groups of Hasidim were strolling. The satin caftans and even those of cotton—the old and ragged, as well as the new ones—were glittering like mirrors. And the little fires which surged between the grasses would tease and touch and be reflected from the holiday garments. It seemed as if lights were dancing around every Hasid with exaltation and tenderness. And all of the Hasidim gazed—with wonderfully thirsty eyes—up at the rebbe's porch. I could feel these eyes draw sustenance from the rebbe's face. The more of this radiance they drew, the higher rose their song. Higher, always higher—ever more joyously, ever more holy.

Each of these groups sang its own song. But all of their tunes, all of the voices, mingled in the air. A single melody that rose to where the rebbe stood, as if all of his disciples were singing one song.

And all things sang. The skies were singing, the celestial spheres, and the earth beneath. The spirit of the world was singing. Now everything was song.

I thought that I was dissolving into the loving sweetness.

Yet it was not meant to last. . . .

"Time for evening prayer!" the rov suddenly said sharply. And everything vanished.

Quiet!

The veil fell back over my eyes. An ordinary sky above. And

below—everyday pastures, commonplace Hasidim in their torn caftans. Limping fragments of old songs. The little sparks extinguished.

I looked at my rebbe. His face was in darkness.

They came to no agreement. When he returned to Brisk, the rov still was hostile, as he had been before.

But the meeting had one positive result. After this the Brisker Rov stopped his persecution of Hasidim.

Translated by Nathan Halper

Ne'ilah * in Gehenna

The town square . . . an ordinary day, neither a market day nor a day of the fair, a day of drowsy small activity. . . . Suddenly there is heard, coming from just outside the town, approaching nearer and nearer, a wild impetuous clatter, a splutter and splashing of mud, a racket of furious wheels! In-ter-est-ing, think the merchants, wonder who it is? At their booths, at their storefronts, they peer out, curious.

As the galloping horse, the thundering wagon, turn into and careen through the square, they are recognized! The townsfolk recoil, revulsion and fear and anger upon their faces. The informer of the neighboring town is at it again! Posthaste to the capital! God alone knows on whom he is going to do a job now.

Suddenly a stillness falls upon the marketplace. Reluctantly, with loathing, the townsfolk look around. The wagon has come to a halt. The horse is lazily nuzzling in the mire of the wheel ruts. And the informer, fallen from his seat, lies stretched out on the ground!

Well, even an informer has a soul; they can't just let him lie there, so the townsfolk rush forward to the body, motionless in the mud. Dead—like every other corpse! Finished! The members of the Burial Society make ready to do the last rites for the deceased.

Horse and wagon are sold to pay for the funeral expenses; the informer is duly interred; and those little imps of dispatch, who crop up just there where you won't see them, snatch up his soul and bear it off to the watchers of the gates of Gehenna.

There, at the gates, the informer is detained while the fiend of reception, he who keeps hell's register of admission and dis-

*Ne'ilah—the last of the five services held on the Day of Atonement.

charge wearily puts the questionnaire to him and as wearily, with his leaking pen, enters the answers: Who, When, How.

The informer—in hell he feels cut down to size—respectfully answers: Born in such and such a place; became a son-in-law in such and such a place; was supported by father-in-law for such and such a number of years; abandoned wife and children; pursued in such and such places his chosen profession, until, his time having come, as he was passing with horse and wagon through the marketplace of Ladam——

At the mention of this name the fiend of reception, in the middle of a yawn, pricks up his ears. "How do you say it? La-ha——"

"Ladam!"*

The fiend goes red in the face, little lights of puzzlement twinkle in his eyes, and he turns to his assistants. "Ever hear of such a town?"

The assistant imps shrug their shoulders. Their tongues stuck between their teeth, they shake their heads. "Never heard of it!"

"*Is* there such a town?"

Now in the records of Gehenna every community has its own file, and these files are all alphabetically arranged, and every letter has its own filing cabinet. So a careful search is made through L—Lublin, Lemberg, Leipzig, they're all there—but no Ladam!

"Still, it's there," the informer persists, "a town in Poland."

"Contemporary or historical?"

"Founded twenty years ago. The baron built it up. It boasts, in fact, two fairs a year. Has a synagogue, a house of study, a bathhouse. Also two Gentile taverns."

Again the registrar addresses himself to his assistants. "Any of you remember—did we ever get anybody here from Ladam?"

"Never!"

Impatiently they turn to the informer. "Don't they ever die in this Ladam of yours?"

"And why shouldn't they?" he answers Jewish-wise, by returning a question. "Close, congested hovels that stifle you. A bathhouse where you can't catch your breath. The whole town—a morass!"

---

*The original Hebrew has L H D M, which are the initial letters of the phrase *lo hayu devarim m'olam*, meaning, "these things never were," "a pure fiction."

The informer is now in his element.

"Never die!" he continues. "Why, they have a completely laid-out cemetery! It's true that the Burial Society will flay you for the costs of burial before they bring you to eternal rest, but still they do have a cemetery. And not so long ago they had an epidemic too."

The interrogation at an end, due judgment is rendered concerning the informer, and concerning the town of Ladam due investigation is instituted. A town twenty years old, a town with an epidemic in its history—and not one soul landed in Gehenna! This was a matter one couldn't let drop.

The imps of inquiry are sent forth diligently to search the thing out.

They return.

True!

And they report as follows: That in the realm of Poland there is indeed a town called Ladam; that it is still extant; that it boasts its tally of good deeds and admits to a quantum (greater) of misdeeds; that its economy presents the usual occupations and the usual struggle; and that the spirit of evil representing hell's interest in the said place, he too is not unemployed.

Why, then, have there never been any candidates for Gehenna from Ladam?

Because Ladam has a cantor! There lies the explanation! And what a cantor! Himself he's nothing! But his voice! A voice for singing, so sweet, so poignant-sweet, that when it weeps it penetrates right into hearts of iron, through and through; it melts them to wax! He has but to ascend the prayer stand, this cantor, and lift his voice in prayer, and behold, the entire congregation of Ladam is made one mass of repentance, wholehearted repentance, all its officers and members reduced, as if one person, to singlehearted contrition! With what result? With the result that, Up There, Ladam's sins are nullified, voided, made of no effect! With the result that for Ladam the gates of paradise—because of this cantor—are forthwith flung apart! When somebody comes before those gates and says he's from Ladam—no further questions asked!

It was easy to see that, with such a cantor in the vicinity, Gehenna would have to operate in Ladam at a loss. Accordingly the matter was taken over by That Certain Party himself! Head of hell, he would deal with the cantor personally.

So he orders that there be brought to him alive from the regions mundane a crowing Calcutta rooster, with comb of fiery red.

Done.

The Calcutta cock, frightened and bewildered in its new roost, lies motionless on the satanic altar, while he—may his name be blotted out!—circles around and around it, squats down before it, never taking his eye off it, his evil eye upon that bright red crest; winds around it, encircles it, until, the spell having worked, the red crest blenches and pales and grows white as chalk. But suddenly, in the midst of this sorcery, an ominous rumbling is heard from Up There. The Holy One, blessed be He, waxes wrathful! So he—may his name be blotted out!—in alarm desists, but not before he spits out a farewell curse.

"Cock-crow, begone! Begone his singing voice! Until the hour of his death!"

Against whom he really launched this curse, you, of course, have already surmised, and indeed even before the blood returned to the crest of the comb of the Calcutta rooster, the cantor of Ladam was minus his voice. Smitten in the throat. Couldn't bring out a note.

The source and origin of this affliction was known, but known, naturally, only to truly holy Jews, and even of these perhaps not to all. But what could one do? One couldn't, of course, explain it; the cantor just wouldn't understand. It was one of those things. Now, had the cantor himself been a man of good deeds, worth, and piety, one might perhaps have interceded for him, hammered at the gates of heaven, clamored against injustice, but when the cantor was, as all knew, a man of insignificant merit, a trifle in the scales, a nothing, why, then . . .

So the cantor himself went knocking at the doors of the great rabbis, soliciting their help, imploring their intervention before the heavenly throne.

To no avail. It couldn't be done.

At last, winning his way into the court of the *tzaddik* of Apt, he clings to the *tzaddik*, won't be sundered from him, weeps, begs, and, unless and until he is helped, won't budge a step from the court. It is a most pitiable thing to see. Not being able to suffer the poor cantor's plight any longer, the *tzaddik* of Apt reluctantly decided to tell the cantor the irrevocable, but not without mixing in it some measure of consolation. "Know, Cantor," he says, "that your hoarseness will persist until your death, but know also that when, at the hour of your death, you come to say the Prayer of Repentance, you will say it with a voice so clear, you will sing it with a voice so musical, that it will resound through all the corridors of heaven!"

"And until then?"

"Lost!"

The cantor still refuses to depart. "But Rabbi, why? Rabbi, what for?"

He persists so long that at last the *tzaddik* tells him the whole story—informer, rooster, and curse.

"If that's the case," the cantor cries out in all his hoarseness, "if that's the case, I—will—have—my—revenge!" And he dashes out.

"Revenge? How and from whom?" the *tzaddik* calls after him.

But the cantor is gone.

This was on a Tuesday, some say Wednesday; and that Thursday, in the evening, when the fishermen of Apt, out on the river to catch their fish for the Sabbath, drew up their nets, they drew forth the drowned body of the cantor of Ladam!

A suicide! From the little bridge over the river! For the saying of the Prayer of Repentance his singing voice had indeed come back to him, even as the *tzaddik* of Apt had promised, the learned *tzaddik* interpreting the words of That Certain Party and stressing them, "*until* the hour of his death"—but not *the* hour of his death.

Yet despite this assurance the cantor—and this was his revenge, as you will soon see—purposely, in that last hour, both on the bridge and in the water, refrained from saying the Prayer of Repentance!

No sooner is the cantor buried, according to the rite of suicides, than the imps are at his soul and to Gehenna he is brought. At the gates the questions are put to him, but he refuses to answer. He is prodded with a pitchfork, stimulated with glowing coals—still he keeps silent, won't answer.

"Take him as is!"

For these questionings in hell are but a matter of form; hell's own agents have all these years lain in wait for the unsuspecting cantor; hell knows in advance the answers to Who, When, What for. The cantor is led to his proper place. A caldron seethes and boils before him.

But here, here the cantor at last permits himself the privilege

of his voice. Clear and ringing he sings it forth.
"Yit-ga-da-al. . . ."
    The *Kaddish of Ne'ilah!*
    He intones it, he sings it, and in singing his voice grows
bolder, stronger . . . melts away . . . revives . . . is rapturous . . .
glorious as in the world aforetime . . . no, better . . . sweeter . . .
in the heart, deeper . . . from the depths . . . clamorous . . .
resurgent. . . .
    Hushed are all the boiling caldrons from which up to now
there had issued a continual sound of weeping and wailing;
hushed, until, after a while, from these same caldrons, an an-
swering hum is heard. The caldron lids are lifted, heads peer
out, burned lips murmur accompaniment.
    The fiends of calefaction stationed at the caldrons, refuse, of
course, to make the responses. Bewildered, abashed, they stand
there as if lost, one with his fagots for the fire, another with his
steaming ladle, a third with his glowing rake. Faces twisted . . .
mouths agape . . . tongues lolling . . . eyes bulging from the
sockets . . . Some fall into epileptic fits and roll, convulsed and
thrashing, on the ground.
    But the cantor continues with his *Ne'ilah.*
    The cantor continues, and the fires under the caldrons di-
minish and fade and go out. The dead begin to crawl forth from
their caldrons.
    The cantor sings on, and the congregation of hell in undertone
accompanies him, prays with him; and passage by passage, as
the prayer is rendered, hurt bodies are healed, become whole,
torn flesh unites, skin is renewed, the condemned dead grow
pure.
    Yes, when the cantor comes to the verse where he cries out,
"Who quickeneth the dead," and hell's poor souls respond
"Amen, Amen," it is as if a resurrection, there and then, is taking
place!
    For such a clamor arises at this Amen that the heavens above
are opened, and the repentance of the wicked reaches to the
heaven of heavens, to the seventh heaven, and comes before the
throne itself. And, it being a moment of grace and favor, the
sinners, now saints, suddenly grow wings. One after the other
out of Gehenna they fly . . . to the very gates of paradise.
    Thereafter there remained in Gehenna only the fiends, rolling
in their convulsions, and the cantor, stock-still at his stand. He

did not leave. True, here in hell he had brought, as he had brought on earth, his congregation to repentance, but he himself had not known a true repentance. That unsaid Prayer of Repentance . . . that matter of suicide. . . .

In the course of time Gehenna was filled again, and although additional suburbs were built, it still remains crowded.

Translated by A. M. Klein

Devotion Without End

There once dwelt in Safed a Jew of great wealth and good fortune, who traded in jewels, diamonds, and other precious stones. He was truly a man of great wealth, not like the upstarts of our day.

This Jew lived in a palace of his own, with windows that shone like gleaming eyes upon the Sea of Galilee; and about this palace bloomed a magnificent garden with all manner of beautiful trees and fruits. Songbirds sang in the sky, and on the earth there grew aromatic herbs that were a joy to behold and of much use in healing. Wide paths, strewn with golden sand, wound through the garden, and over these paths the crowns of the trees wove into one another to form a canopy of shade. Little arbors in which one could rest lay scattered along the edges of the garden, and in the ponds, which glistened like mirrors, there swam the rarest and whitest of swans. It was an earthly paradise.

The Jew had his own mules and camels with which to cross the desert; and for sailing the sea he had his own ship, with his own crew and captain. Would that all Israel knew such blessings!

Nor was this Jew miserly with his wealth. He married his children into rabbinical families and into the families of the learned in both Babylon and Palestine; he sent his sons to study Torah, and when the time came for his sons to leave he would joyfully give to each of them his share of the inheritance. In time there remained at home only his youngest child, the beloved Sarah, whom he treasured above all others.

Sarah was exceedingly beautiful, a maiden soft in heart and sweet in temper.

And when the time came he presented his youngest daughter with a wonderful gift, brought from the Babylonian yeshivah: a youth named Chiya. The head of the Babylonian yeshivah wrote to the rabbi of Safed that Chiya was no less than "the crown of my head" and "the crown of the yeshivah." And as for lineage, Chiya's was the finest, the very finest in Israel.

Rumors soon spread through the world that Chiya came from

a princely line; but the records of his descent had been destroyed in the siege of Babylon, where Chiya had lost mother and father, brothers and sisters, and had himself been saved only through a miracle. Of this none ever knew for certain, since Reb Chiya, in his great modesty, never spoke of it. But it is known that when the people saw the lad Chiya walking in the street they would gaze upon him as upon a radiant picture, and some would even stop to recite a blessing over his loveliness. For Chiya had a truly royal face: the Divine Presence shone down upon him.

Chiya settled with his father-in-law at Safed, devoting himself entirely to the study of Torah. Soon, however, his life of seclusion and repose came to an end, for his father-in-law died shortly after the wedding. The young man had no choice but to take over the worldly affairs of the family and to make journeys to every corner of the earth. So it was that he became one of the greatest merchants of his time.

But this, God forbid, did not tempt him to relinquish his study of the Torah. When Reb Chiya rode upon his camel in the desert, a servant would lead the animal by the reins, while he kept his eyes fastened upon the sacred book that lay in his hand. And in his ship there was a separate cabin where he would sit in privacy, giving himself unto Torah, both to that which is revealed and that which is unrevealed.

Reb Chiya even found time to devote himself to the Seven Wisdoms of the old sheiks whom he met on his journeys in the desert: to the science of medicine, to the language of the birds and the beasts, even to astrology.

His deeds of charity were numberless, and wherever he went his hand gave freely to those in need. Not only did he put aside a tenth of his earnings for the poor, he also ransomed captive Jews of whose plight he heard while traveling in distant lands. And so it came about that Reb Chiya performed many a great deed in behalf of the people of Israel.

Since Reb Chiya dealt in diamonds and pearls, he met many princes and their ministers during his travels, and through his beauty and honesty—or perhaps it was still more through his wisdom—he gained favor in their eyes. These princes and ministers had faith in his word, and were always ready to grant him mercy for a fellow Jew.

Thus did Reb Chiya become a spokesman for his people. Merely by giving his word, he could obtain the annulment of evil decrees, save Jews from the chains and lashes to which they had been unjustly condemned, and more than once snatch a victim from the hangman's rope. Many, too, were the souls that he rescued from the still worse fate of forced apostasy.

During the lengthy months and years that Reb Chiya was absent from home, his good wife Sarah would maintain the kind of household that did honor to a man of his standing. Reb Chiya had complete faith in her. He knew that the hungry would leave her door sated and the thirsty refreshed. And he knew that Sarah would raise their only daughter in the ways of piety and goodness.

So, indeed, it was. The palace was always full of guests, the poor and the learned, beggars and rabbis. Whenever the heads of the yeshivahs traveled abroad to seek help, they would stop at the House of Reb Chiya's Wife—for so it had come to be called —and there she would receive them with generosity and joy. She would ask for one thing only: that they place their hands on the head of Miriam, her daughter, and give her their blessing. Nor were the blessings in vain, for Miriam was like a gift from heaven, a child of loveliness. All of Safed basked in her beauty and goodness, saying, "Reb Chiya's daughter is radiant as the sun. She moves with the grace and charm of Queen Esther."

But the ways of God are beyond understanding, and as King Solomon once said, "Whomever God loves, him does He chastise." Often the Almighty tests the pious by visiting many sorrows upon them to see how deep and strong is their faith. Be that as it may, the virtuous Sarah suddenly fell sick. Reb Chiya received the news in a distant corner of the earth, and in his heart knew that the worst had come. Quickly he abandoned all his affairs and hastened home over mountains and valleys, seas and deserts. Many were the obstacles he encountered: mules and camels fell beneath him in the desert, the storms of the sea beat wildly against his ship—yet God did not forsake him. Reb Chiya overcame all these troubles and reached his home in safety. Sarah was close to her end. When the pious wife looked upon her husband, she gathered together all her strength and sat up in bed, murmuring her gratitude to God for listening to her prayer and allowing her to see once more the face of her beloved husband. She turned to Reb Chiya and consoled him, saying that she accepted the coming of death in a spirit of readiness; and then she spoke to him of their daughter Miriam. Reb Chiya vowed that he would be both father and mother to the child, that no strange hands would be allowed to bend or twist or, heaven forbid, break their tender plant. And the dying Sarah promised that in the world above she would not forget her husband Chiya or her daughter Miriam; she would beg the heavenly powers to send their daughter a husband of honor and virtue. If ever there should be any perplexity with regard to the child, she, Sarah, would beg permission to appear before Chiya in a dream and there tell him what must be done. So it was that she bid farewell to Reb Chiya. She recited the Shema Yisrael once more, and then she cast loving eyes upon the face of Reb Chiya and begged him to accept the will of heaven. She slid down from her pillow, drew up her feet, turned toward the wall, and rendered her spotless soul unto God.

No sooner were the thirty days of mourning at an end than Reb Chiya, without a moment's hesitation, disposed of his pearls and rubies and diamonds and settled once again to a life of study and good deeds. He transformed his palace into a yeshivah, and from among the Jews of Safed and its vicinity he brought together the most gifted youths, whom he taught each day another portion of holy wisdom. These youths drank from his wisdom with eagerness, and those who were poor he maintained in his palace, lodging two or three to a splendid room and clothing them as if they were the sons of the wealthy. Nothing could escape Reb Chiya's foresight: he even thought to give them pocket money, so that the poorest among them might enjoy an occasional innocent pleasure and not be shamed before their wealthier companions.

Whenever one of these poorer students reached the age for marriage, Reb Chiya would send messengers in search of a suitable bride. He would provide the dowry, the wedding clothes, and at least half the cost of the wedding; he would conduct the bridegroom to the wedding canopy; and he would himself give the wedded pair his blessing. As for his beloved daughter, Miriam, he hoped that the day would come when there would appear for her a youth among youths, one who would find favor in the eyes of man and in the eyes of God.

It was on this theme that he once wrote to the head of the Babylonian yeshivah, a sage with whom he corresponded on all matters holy and profane. He wrote in that flowery Hebrew which is only proper for such subjects, and as we transpose it here into profane Yiddish it must lose much of its sweetness:

"With the help of Him whose name is sweet I have planted a lovely garden (the yeshivah) in which many trees bear fruit (the students), and once the fruit ripens (the students who reach the age of marriage), I seek to find for it a worthy buyer (a good father-in-law) and tell him to say the blessing over the fruit (the wedding ceremony). And if God will look upon me with favor and show me a citron without blemish, that citron shall be for my beloved Miriam, long may she live."

To which the head of the Babylonian yeshivah replied in his usual concise way: "Can it be that in your yeshivah there are no scholars of sufficient distinction?"

And then it was that Reb Chiya hinted that something other than scholarship was troubling him.

"The Torah," he wrote in his metaphorical style, "is like a stream, yet not all streams have their source in Paradise—not all men study Torah in a spirit of purity. One man studies Torah only to slake his vanity: his sole desire is to surpass and humiliate his fellows. A second studies for the sake of reputation: his desire is not to honor the Torah but that the torah honor him. A third brings to the Torah still another kind of lust: he enjoys disputation for its own sake; his delight consists not in reaching toward the wisdom of God but in displaying the cleverness of his mind, his little novelties of interpretation, his paltry twisting of texts. To prove his cleverness he is even ready to distort the visible meaning of the Torah. And others are still more gross: the Torah becomes for them a spade with which to dig the ground, to find a wealthy father-in-law, a fat living, and, at the end, an inheritance! Even if a student may be found who desires learning for its own sake—still his soul is marred by some stain, some imperfection. Of citrons there are many, but Reb Chiya desires for his Miriam only one that is pure within and pure without. Nor is that so easy to find, for the heart of man is deep and devious. As the Talmud says, honor a man and beware of him."

Again the head of the Babylonian yeshivah replied with his customary terseness: "Search and thou shalt find."

But where is one to search?

Reb Chiya used to say: "One might imagine that a man's true character could be discovered in his eyes. The soul lies imprisoned in his body, and the Creator of the Universe, in his infinite mercy, has built two windows in the walls of his prison. These are the eyes, and through them the soul looks out upon the world and may, in turn, be seen by the world. But these windows, alas, have curtains; and a man whose soul is flawed tries to keep it from sight—even as a bride with a defect is kept from sight before the wedding. And just when the soul is ready to let itself be seen, he lowers the curtain, presumably from modesty."

It would be easier, claimed Reb Chiya, to recognize a man's character by his voice. And about this Reb Chiya had a theory of his own.

"Man may be compared to an earthen pot. The ordinary soul is but a piece of broken pottery, while the extraordinary soul is like an earthen pot which can receive the waters of the Torah without losing a drop. But this is possible only when the pottery is whole and uncracked. How then can one be certain that the pottery is not flawed, even if flawed so slightly as to escape the eye? You need only tap the pot with your finger, and if its ring is clear and full, all is well. If not . . .

"A man who is not whole may have a voice that is high or low, a voice that is broken or a voice that trembles; but he will never have one that is clear and true. Between a man and a pot, however, there is this difference: if you tap a man whose voice is defective, he has the ability to imitate, in the manner of a parrot, the voice of a stranger. Have you sometimes heard from a distance the voice of a bird and then, upon coming nearer, discovered that it was the mimicry of a parrot?"

These notions Reb Chiya would put to the test in the following manner.

It was his custom to teach the day's lesson in the morning. Later, in the afternoon, he would release his students to enjoy the shade of the trees, taste the fruit, and say the blessing over it. As they walked through the garden they would rehearse the lesson of the day or discuss some obscure problem of the Torah; or even if they engaged in some innocent chatter on a secular topic, that too was no fault. Reb Chiya would shut himself away in his study and pore over the unrevealed portions of the Torah. Over a window of this room looking out upon the garden, there hung a thick silken curtain. From time to time Reb Chiya would drop his spectacles, lay them on the prayer book before him, cover it with his scarf, and on top of all place his little snuffbox. He would walk over to the window and stand near the curtain, listening to the voices of his students, who were walking about in pairs or in groups and talking freely to one another.

What they said he neither could nor wished to hear; only the sound of their voices reached him, never the words. And as the months passed Reb Chiya, never once hearing a true voice, fell into a deep sadness.

Once he went so far as to complain. "Master of the Universe, the birds in the garden that have but the souls of animals sing thy praises; my pupils, each of whom has a unique soul, study the Torah. Yet, why is it that the voice of the birds is pure and whole, while the voices of my students . . ."

Reb Chiya did not finish; it would be unseemly to speak ill of his own pupils. But the sadness in his heart remained.

From time to time new pupils arrived, and with them new voices, yet there was not a voice of perfect quality among them.

Once he stopped his daughter, Miriam, looked upon her with love and pity, and asked, "My daughter, do you ever visit your mother's grave?"

"Yes," she answered.

"And what do you pray for at your mother's grave?"

Lifting her faithful eyes, she replied, "I pray for your health, my father. At times you seem so sad, and I, alas, know not how to gladden you. She, my mother, knew how. So I pray to her that she shall teach my heart, or tell me in a dream."

Reb Chiya patted her silken cheeks and told her, "My health, praise be to God, is as it should be. There is something else that you must pray for at your mother's grave."

"And that is——?"

"Beg her to help bring to pass that which I have in mind for you."

"I shall, my father."

It happened once, before the evening prayer, that Reb Chiya heard a loud quarrel in a distant part of the house. He could hear two voices, the angry voice of his assistant and the other, young and strange. The unfamiliar voice astonished Reb Chiya: this was the voice for which he had hoped and prayed. Closing the book he had been studying, Reb Chiya heard how the pleading young voice was slowly drowned out by the wrathful voice of his assistant. Reb Chiya rapped on his table to call his assistant, who came running, frightened and alarmed. His aged face was still pale, his eyes flashed darts of fire, his nostrils still danced—so angry had he been.

Reb Chiya warned him: anger is a sin more terrible than idolatry.

"No, Rabbi," the old man said sulkily, "the Messiah must be here—that's the only explanation for such insolence from a mere youth."

"Well, all right—but what does he want?"

"A trifle—just to be admitted to your yeshivah!"

"Well?"

"So I ask him, 'Do you know the Talmud?' He answers, 'No!' 'Mishnah, at least?' 'No,' he says again. So I try a joke. 'Can you at least say the prayers?' And again, 'No!' He bursts into tears. What then? Well, he can read the words of the prayers but has forgotten their meaning. 'Numskull, what do you want from us?' He wants Reb Chiya. 'Why?' To beg you to let him sit in the yeshivah and listen to the lessons, so that perhaps God will help him remember."

"That means he knew and forgot," mused Reb Chiya. "He's sick. Why be angry?"

"Why be angry? I say to him, 'All right, I'll let you see Reb Chiya.' But the youth is dressed in rags, with a rope around his loins, and he carries a staff in his hand, as if he were a thief—a peeled branch of an almond tree. I tell him, 'You can see Reb Chiya, but first change your clothes. Have you others?' He neither has nor wishes to. He's not allowed to, he says. 'At least put your staff away.' Nor that either. He's not allowed to part with it, neither in the day nor at night. He sleeps with it!"

Reb Chiya, realizing that this must be a penitent, said, "Send him in."

A pale slender youth entered, dressed just as the assistant had said, and remained standing at the door.

Reb Chiya asked him to come nearer, extended a hand of welcome, and prevented him from kneeling or kissing his hand. Seeing that the youth did not lift his eyes, Reb Chiya asked, "My son, why do you not look at me? Are you hiding your soul from my eyes?"

"Yes, Rabbi," answered the youth, "my soul is sinful, my shame is great."

Replied Reb Chiya, "Our sages say that no man may speak against himself. I ask you to lift up your eyes."

The youth obeyed. And Reb Chiya, looking into his eyes, was seized with a violent trembling: before him he saw a soul that had been cursed.

"Tell me, my son, who has cursed you?"

"The head of the Jerusalem yeshivah."

Knowing that the head of the Jerusalem yeshivah had died only recently, Reb Chiya asked, "When?"

"Two months ago."

Correct, thought Reb Chiya. Two months ago he was still alive. Aloud he asked, "Why?"

"About that I have been directed to confess to you."

"Good. And your name?"

"Chananiah."

"Well, Chananiah," said Reb Chiya, rising, "let us say the evening prayers and then you will be shown your place at the table. After you have eaten, go to the garden, where I shall hear out your story."

Reb Chiya took the youth by the hand and led him to the little synagogue by the side of the yeshivah.

And while they walked, these were the thoughts that ran through Reb Chiya's head: so young and such a voice . . . and a penitent . . . a curse in his eyes . . . wondrous are the ways of the Almighty.

It was late in the evening when Reb Chiya and Chananiah walked through the garden. Reb Chiya would cast glances at the sky, seeking some sign or omen; but the sky was veiled with a gray and silent mist; a night without a moon, without stars. Only the windows of the palace gleamed with little lights, and by these Reb Chiya led the youth Chananiah to an arbor.

Reb Chiya began, "There is a hebrew proverb, *'D'aga b'lev ish—yeshina.'* "

"What does that mean, Rabbi?"

"It means: *d'aga*—sorrow (Chananiah repeated each word); *b'lev*—in the heart; *ish* of a man; *yeshina*—he shall tell another. That is, a man with a heart of sorrow shall pour it out to another."

And though the youth understood only the translation his pale face began to flush, as if he had fainted and only now was his soul gradually returning to his body.

Reb Chiya, filled with pity for the youth, told him, "Open your lips, my son, and may your words enter the light. Speak to me, my son."

And this was the strange tale that Chananiah told him.

The youth had been born in Jerusalem, the son of a wealthy widow who dealt in spices. Of her two children, the woman favored Chananiah over his elder sister Esther, for it was he who would someday say Kaddish in her memory, and he, moreover, who quickly showed himself to be a prodigy.

Even when Esther reached the age of sixteen the mother remained untroubled by the fact that her daughter had not yet married. And when the neighbors reminded her that the time for marriage had come, the mother had a ready answer: "The girl's hair has not even turned gray." The mother's heart was wholly given over to her son Chananiah. She hired excellent tutors for the boy, and since, as a distant relative of the head of the Jerusalem yeshivah, she had entry into his house, she would bring Chananiah to be examined by him every few Sabbaths.

The youth impressed the head of the yeshivah greatly, and the mother would be beside herself with joy as she stood listening near the door, peering through a crack and seeing how the rabbi pinched the boy's cheek fondly and gave him the best apple from the Sabbath fruit bowl. Still greater was her joy when the rabbi's wife told her that the boy would be accepted by the Jerusalem yeshivah—though to this she did not agree, for she was unwilling to part from her son. She wished to keep her darling at home, so that she could entrust her shop to a neighbor for a moment and hurry into the house to embrace her child. She therefore engaged a more learned scholar who would study with the boy at home.

And it was this teacher who caused her downfall.

He was one of the false scholars who come to the Torah not for its own sake or from love of God but out of a lust to shine in their own right; and he soon led Chananiah along his false path. He taught the boy nothing but the devices of sophistry, the art of negating all things; and in the boy's heart he planted the bitter herbs of pride and presumption. Chananiah soon learned all of his tricks, for such knowledge is, in truth, mere trickery, not the wisdom of the Torah—it was not this that was meant at Sinai. But neither the mother nor the neighbors understood this; and so they praised the boy still more. And the mother—for what can one expect from a foolish woman?—swelled with pride.

The time came when Chananiah had absorbed all that his teacher could offer, and he told his mother that he could now study on his own. The foolish woman felt that the gates of heaven had opened for her.

Chananiah now trod the false path by himself, engaging in

disputes with the students at the yeshivah and with older scholars, whom he always put to shame and made seem mere ignoramuses. So it continued until word reached the head of the yeshivah, who said, "Youthful foolishness! But he will grow out of it," and then sent word to Chananiah's mother that she should punish the boy. "A mother," he added, "is allowed to."

But instead the mother gave Chananiah a kiss and bought him a costly present.

Encouraged, Chananiah strayed still further, running about in all the synagogues to display his tricks. He would interrupt the studies of pupils, asking them questions about the passages they were reading and then destroying the answers they gave him. So it continued until the student would become bewildered, and Chananiah had proved to everyone that the student was worthless.

Sometimes it happened that when a youth was explaining a passage of the Torah or a scholar was preaching—and this hardly before the speaker had finished—Chananiah would spring onto the pulpit and ridicule the explanation or cut the sermon into ribbons, as if with a scissors, ripping through it as through a cobweb and making the other seem a mere fool.

Again, word was brought to the head of the yeshivah, who now issued a stricter judgment: "Tell his mother that I have asked her to punish him severely." And again, instead of beating Chananiah, she rewarded him with kisses and gifts, so that he went still further along the paths of evil. When the word was brought once more to the head of the yeshivah he sighed, hesitating to do that which should be left to a mother. But once he was told how the mother responded, he ordered that Chananiah be brought to him. The youth came, flaming with pride. And when the head of the yeshivah began to speak of Torah, he interrupted with needling questions, questions upon questions that were meant to show the prowess of his mind.

But the head of the yeshivah was truly a saintly man, and without a trace of anger he quietly replied "Hear me out, Chananiah! All your knowledge can do is to negate—you have nothing but the power of saying 'no'—which means that you do not possess the Torah whole. For the Torah is made up of two parts, the one that allows and the other that forbids, the one that says 'Thou shalt' and the other 'Thou shalt not.' And you,

Chananiah, have only the second half of the Torah. More than half you shall never have. And here is proof: say something of your own that carries the power of 'yes.' "

Chananiah was silent; his strength lay solely in destruction. He tried to justify himself. "But this I did not learn from my teacher."

Answered the head of the yeshivah, "Your teacher, Chananiah, is dead, and the fires of hell have wrapped themselves around him. His kind of Torah cannot save him. He will burn, Chananiah, until you root out from your heart the weeds he planted. You must take pity both on your soul and on his; come, repent, study the Torah in its purity."

Chananiah quickly ran off to the cemetery to see whether his teacher was really dead. There he was told, "Yes, the funeral took place yesterday," and they led him to the grave. He saw that overnight the grave had been covered with foul and ugly weeds. And Chananiah, knowing what this meant, decided to repent.

But something happened to interfere, alas, with Chananiah's resolve.

There lived in Jerusalem in those days a retired butcher, to whom the Jewish authorities had once sent a learned Jew to see whether he sold defiled meat as kosher; and when this learned Jew tried to carry out his task faithfully and appeared unannounced at a slaughtering, the butcher seized an ax and hurled it at his head. It was a miracle that the man survived; and a great commotion followed in the city. The Jewish authorities announced that the butcher's meat was not kosher, worse even than the flesh of swine. But since the butcher had by now become wealthy from his illicit trade, he closed his shop and became a usurer and an informer for the government. He complained against the Jewish authorities, who were thereupon cast into prison and banished. And since he no longer sold meat to his fellow Jews there was nothing they could do to him. They merely thanked God that this scoundrel had done no more damage than he had and hoped that he might now be quiet.

The wealthy butcher, who possessed the heart of a miser, did not enjoy his wealth; he neither ate nor drank, he dressed shabbily, and he raised fierce dogs to keep beggars from his door. He had no sons and but one daughter, whose name was Hannah. When this only daughter was born, his wife, a good and pious woman, fully realized the evil of her husband's ways and prayed to God that her womb be closed, for she did not desire sons who would follow in their father's footsteps. So it came to pass; she had but one daughter, and all her efforts to lead her husband to the path of virtue failed. As her life became unbearable to her, she prayed for an early death; and this prayer too was granted. Before she died she begged her relatives to bury her in secrecy, so that her husband would not know the place of her grave.

Thus it happened that the tyrant became a widower. And since no father would entrust him with a daughter, he did not remarry but lived alone with his only child Hannah. By some miracle he loved his daughter with all his heart and was ready to bestow upon her all the pleasures he denied himself—even though money was dearer to him than his soul. But Hannah refused everything, living by her mother's command that she accept nothing from her father but bread and water. Nor did the girl need expensive clothes, for she never left her father's house, not wishing to hear him cursed and abused in the streets of Jerusalem. Yet the less she desired the use of his money, the more did the father wish to heap favors upon her.

When he saw that his daughter remained stubborn in her ways the father decided: one favor she will accept, a husband who is a great scholar.

As soon as Hannah approached the age for marriage the father began to seek a husband for her. He wanted a scholar surpassing all other scholars; he hired marriage brokers to scour the land, and he himself rushed through Jerusalem, searching in all the yeshivahs and promising a generous dowry to the youth who might be chosen. But it was all in vain. No one wished to be related to the wealthy butcher—and as for his daughter, her true worth remained unknown.

The man grew angry, and angrier still when a marriage broker once told him to put aside his pride and make the best of things by accepting the one man who was available, a poor carpenter who earned his bread honestly and who wanted Hannah for her own sake.

The wealthy butcher hit upon the plan of sending through the length and breadth of the land, especially to the distant corners where his name was not known, two poverty-stricken scholars whom he paid for two years in advance. Being poor, the two scholars could not refuse, and so they traveled the length and breadth of Israel—but to no avail.

Nor was it difficult to discover the reason for their failure. They spoke of a dowry and of maintenance for the future husband and of gifts, but of Hannah's father they said not a word. When they were asked about him they pretended not to hear, for they were honest men who did not wish to lie. And thus it became clear that something was very wrong, and no one wanted the match.

The two years passed, and now, before the gates of Jerusalem, the two learned Jews stood empty-handed, trembling with fear. Had they not left behind them wives and children they might have gone to some other country, for they knew that their employer would refuse to believe them and would think they had failed to do as he had told them. Perhaps he would even go so far as to turn them over to the government. The two learned Jews gave way to lamentations.

And as they sat before the gates of Jerusalem, lamenting their fate, they were accosted by a poor youth dressed in sackcloth, with a hempen rope around his loins and a staff cut from an almond tree in his hand; and this youth came to them, greeted them, asked if they wanted to drink, and inquired why they sat in such dejection; and he told them that he lived in the nearby desert and knew of a well from which they could drink. If they wished he would lead them. But the two learned Jews were not thirsty; they were worried. They asked the youth who he was, and he answered that he was a homeless orphan, living apart from all other men and subsisting on wild grasses.

"And have you no wish to study Torah?"

But he did study Torah, he replied. Every night, when darkness came over the desert, an old man appeared before him and taught him the Torah by word of mouth. He could see this old man from afar, his eyes sparkling like the stars in heaven and his white beard shining like snow, and each night the old man sat beside him, teaching him both Torah and its commentaries.

When they questioned the youth to see if he were truthful, pearls of wisdom seemed to fall from his lips. Then they asked him why he had abandoned the desert and come to sit by the gates of Jerusalem, and he answered with simple honesty that on the previous night the old man had bade him farewell, saying that they had met for the last time, and had directed him to the holy city where he would find both bride and fortune. "And I must obey the old man," added the youth.

As soon as the two learned Jews heard this story they were filled with joy and said to the youth, "Come with us, we know the bride for you." And he went with them.

They took him directly to the wealthy butcher and said, "Do not be concerned with the appearance of this youth. For he is truly wise: Elijah the Prophet has taught him in the wilderness." Without delay or question, the rich man accepted the youth, and fearful that a long delay might result in someone's casting an evil eye or at least spreading malicious gossip, he arranged for a marriage in two weeks. First of all he took the rags off the back of the youth and took the staff from his hand, and then he gave him new clothes such as are suitable for the son of a rich man. The old clothes he kept, however, hoping to sell them for a few coppers after the wedding. The news of this match spread quickly through the town, and some said the biggest dog gets the best bone; while others contended that it was the doing of the bride's mother, who had interceded in heaven. Still others remarked that the ways of God are beyond human comprehension.

The two weeks passed without incident and the day of the wedding came near. For the sake of his daughter the old miser forgot his niggardliness and arranged a feast such as the world has seldom seen. And to honor the bridegroom, all the distinguished Jews of Jerusalem came to the wedding, as did also the students of the yeshivah. While the bride was being prepared for the wedding, the bridegroom discoursed among the men on an esoteric point of Torah.

In the other room, the bride has been made ready. The musicians have begun to play. The chief rabbi and the head of the yeshivah, who are to conduct the groom to the canopy, hold candles in readiness for the wedding procession. And from the groom's lips the wisdom of the Torah continues to flow like a river of myrrh and frankincense, while his eyes gleam like the stars of heaven. All stand gaping with admiration, and Chananiah among them, silently, with no thought of envy or contradiction. On the contrary, he rejoices at the thought that he will now have a companion in study, a friend with whom to discuss all matters of learning. And he is flooded with love, a warm love for the bridegroom. He yearns to get up, to embrace him. He begins to move forward—and then the terrible thing happens.

Passing through the crowd, he hears one yeshivah student

tell another, "The bridegroom is a better scholar than Chananiah," and the second one replies, "Of course, Chananiah is a blockhead by comparison." And this proves too much for Chananiah. It seems as if his heart is bursting, as if a wound has opened, as if a serpent has stung him—the Evil One, his own evil spirit. He stops, he rises on tiptoe, he begins suddenly to speak, and from his mouth there pours a stream of pitch and brimstone, contradiction and desecration. He senses that he is betraying his soul, that he is desecrating the wisdom of Elijah the Prophet, the wisdom of the Torah itself, that he is piercing the heart of the Torah with spears and with swords, he is murdering the Torah. Frightened, he wishes to cease, but he cannot—something outside of his will, a devil, speaks through him, something against his will. He sees the bridegroom turn pale with fear, stagger, collapse.

The wedding chamber becomes a living hell. The old miser, enraged, roars like a wounded lion, "Swindled! I've been swindled!" He rushes about like a madman, finds the two learned Jews who were his emissaries, beats them, and tears out their beards. He throws himself upon the musicians, wrenches the instruments from their hands, and smashes them into pieces. He runs to the bride and drags her away from the wedding canopy. He dashes out to another room and comes back with the bridegroom's old clothes: sackcloth, hempen rope, and staff. Tearing the new ones from the bridegroom's back, he hurls the youth into the street, and his clothes after him. The dignitaries of Jerusalem flee in terror. Only Chananiah remains. He stands in the same spot as if paralyzed and hears the old miser scream, "I won't waste this wedding feast! Bring the carpenter! Let him marry my daughter!" And only now does Chananiah manage to escape from the house.

In the street he encounters the head of the yeshivah, who takes him by the hand and says to him, "Chananiah, your evil is enough to destroy a world! Far better that you forget all you have learned."

"It was at this moment," continued Chananiah, "that something snapped in my brain, and I became as empty as a cage from which the birds have fled. The Torah had taken flight from me. I fell at the feet of the head of the yeshivah and begged for atonement, but he could only sigh. 'Who knows if there is any for you?'

"I began to sob wildly, and he pointed to the bridegroom, who stood not far away, bewildered in the strange city.

" 'As a first step,' said the head of the yeshivah, 'you might beg his forgiveness.'

"I was afraid, but he prodded me, 'Go, ask him to go home with you. I will come later.'

"I went to the bridegroom I had shamed, and before I could say a word he ran up to me and cried out, 'You are forgiven, forgiven! The match was not destined for me.'

"I would have preferred a beating, and he comes up to me, his hand on my shoulder, and calls me friend!

" 'But what sort of friendship,' I replied, 'can there be between an ignoramus and a scholar?' He looked at me, amazed, and then I told him of the curse the head of the yeshivah had placed upon my head. And he said to me, 'If ever again there appears before me my old teacher'—he meant Elijah the Prophet—'I will beg him to help you.'

"I brought him to my mother, suffering all the while the agonies of the damned. He spoke to me of Torah and I understood not a word. My heart wept with yearning for the Torah . . . darkness and desolation flooded my soul, as in a ruin at night. And when we came to my mother's house, I fell upon her neck with the cry, 'Mother, Mother, God has punished us. Your son no longer has a word of learning!'

"She cried out in fright, 'What do you mean? Who has cast a spell upon you?'

"And then I told her the whole story, pointing to the bridegroom I had shamed. She wept bitter tears, and my sister Esther turned her face to the wall, weeping. But at this moment there came the head of the yeshivah, and it was to Esther that he spoke first. 'Hear me, my daughter, go to the kitchen and prepare food for this scholar'—pointing to the youth who stood beside me—'and if fortune will shine upon you, he will prove to be your destined mate.'

"With dismay Esther glanced at the shamed bridegroom, but she obeyed the head of the yeshivah.

"And then he turned to my mother and said, 'This is no time for tears. You too have sinned in not providing for Esther and not punishing Chananiah.' And when my mother sobbed still louder, he continued, 'Not tears are needed now, but acts. Will you do as I tell you?'

" 'Yes,' sobbed my mother, 'I shall, I shall!'

" 'First marry Esther to this youth, for he is her destined mate.'

"A cry broke out of my mother's heart. 'This beggar in rags?'

" 'This is the youth to whom Elijah the Prophet taught the Torah. Is that how you obey me?'

" 'Forgive me, Rabbi! I obey, I obey!'

" 'And your son,' he continued, 'must crawl through the lands of exile, until the mercy of the All-Merciful shall be awakened in his behalf. He too will bring you happiness, but later. Esther is the older one!'

" 'And as for you,' he said to me, 'atonement for your dreadful sin might not have been possible had you not been fortunate. The marriage was not a destined one, and what you did has proved to be good for both bride and bridegroom.'

" 'Even the bride?' wondered my mother.

"To which the head of the yeshivah replied, 'It is known that Hannah, the daughter of the old miser, is good and pious. Her saintly mother pleaded for her in heaven and won for her one of the Thirty-Six Secret Saints upon whom the earth rests. And he is the carpenter whom the old miser dragged to the wedding canopy so that his feast might not go to waste. But this you must keep secret until he reveals himself.'

" 'God's miracles,' said my mother, somewhat relieved.

" 'And now,' he said to me and to the bridegroom, 'now, my dear children, each of you must take the other's clothes.'

" 'And you,' he added to me, 'must begin your wanderings in exile. Take the staff and guard it as the apple of your eye. At night, when you sleep, you shall place it beside your head. And I will pray that help may come to you and that the staff may blossom, so that your soul too will blossom, and then you will remember all that you have forgotten. But remember that only then may you wear other garments. And now go, without saying farewell to anyone.'

"I quickly dressed in the clothes of the bridegroom I had shamed, and at the very moment my sister entered with a plate of food. Seeing us now, she dropped the plate in astonishment. It broke with a loud noise, and the head of the yeshivah cried out, 'Mazel tov, mazel tov!'

"More I did not hear, for I was already on my way."

As soon as he left Jerusalem, said Chananiah to Reb Chiya, he lost his way in a desert, where neither bread nor water was to be found. But he knew no desire for bread or for water, and he satisfied the wants of his body with the wild grasses that lay scattered in the desert. Throughout his wanderings he was in

constant danger from the wild beasts, yet they harmed him not.
When he came near them they would growl and then turn from
his path. Chananiah understood that they had no power over
him, for he was not yet fated to die. Once it seemed to him that a
voice called out, "He belongs to . . ." But to whom it was that
he belonged he could not hear.

And so he wandered in exile, through the days and through
the nights, mourning over his youth that was being wasted
without Torah, without a light or a ray for his darkened mind. If
only he could have heard one word of Torah, one word. . . .

Once, continued Chananiah with his story, he poured a handful of sand upon his head and then, in self-castigation, he stood
on one leg, crying out toward heaven, "Torah, Torah." He cried
with earnest devotion, on and on, until the sun sank, and then he
fell to the earth and slept. In his sleep he saw again the head of the
Jerusalem yeshivah, dressed in the clothes of the grave and with a
golden crown upon his head. And the head of the Jerusalem
yeshivah said to Chananiah, "Arise, Chananiah, for the time of
your redemption is at hand. God has heard your prayer, and
Elijah the Prophet has interceded for you. Arise and go forward,
till you reach the city of Safed, where you shall go to the good
man Reb Chiya and make full confession to him of all that you
have done. You shall beg him to let you enter his yeshivah, and
he will not refuse you. And when you reach the age of eighteen,
he will find your destined bride and he will pray for you. His
prayers, you shall remember, are hearkened to in heaven. And
besides that, the ceremony of marriage and the blessings that
follow it will also help you. On the eighth day after the wedding
you will arise in the morning and will see that the staff by your
head has begun to blossom and to sprout almonds; so too will
your soul bloom and sprout. Then you will remember everything
but the evil that was in you, and you will recite for Reb Chiya a
portion of the Torah, but now it will be a Torah pure and without
defilement. Reb Chiya will rejoice in you, but whether you will
live long after that I cannot foretell."

With these words the head of the Jerusalem yeshivah vanished from Chananiah's dream. Chananiah awoke and began his
journey.

"And now, Reb Chiya, I have come to you." So said
Chananiah.

Reb Chiya looked upon him with great sadness and asked,
"How old are you, my son?"

"Seventeen years and ten months."

"To be cut off so young," mused Reb Chiya.

Chananiah raised his big imploring eyes to Reb Chiya's face and pleaded in a voice that was trembling, "Rabbi, will you take me into your yeshivah?"

An empty soul, thought Reb Chiya, a stranger to the Torah —and yet from his throat one hears a voice like King David's violin. Aloud he said, "Sleep now, my son. Tomorrow I shall answer you."

Chananiah left him, and Reb Chiya remained for a while in the arbor, gazing up at the sky and wondering: Is this the youth for whom I have so long been waiting?

But the heavens were clouded and did not speak.

The next morning, once they were alone, Reb Chiya said to Chananiah, "Know, my son, that for my part I am ready to grant your request, but——"

Chananiah began to tremble. "Rabbi," he begged, "let me sit somewhere in a dark corner, at the back, farthest away from you. I will listen only to what you tell your pupils, I will do nothing but listen."

"I am willing," Reb Chiya comforted him, "but I fear that my students, being young and mischievous, may mock you. And let us not delude ourselves—they know a good deal while you, for the time being. . . . The scorn of the learned for the unlearned is large, and you, my son, will suffer."

Joyously Chananiah cried out, "But I must suffer, Rabbi, I should suffer, and the more I am shamed the sooner will my curse be lifted."

"That may be," said Reb Chiya, "but I am afraid your presence will harm the others. For is it not written"—he continued in Hebrew—"that those who shame others before the world shall lose their portion of paradise?"

These words were now beyond Chananiah's understanding, but when Reb Chiya translated them he was still happier. "It means that even if the curse is lifted from my head I shall still have no share of paradise, so that if I study the Torah it can be only for its own sake, without hope of reward."

To Reb Chiya these words were a delight and a balm. But he continued, "They, my pupils, how can I allow them to lose their share of eternal life?"

Chananiah remained silent for a moment and then replied, "And if I forgave them beforehand?"

Reb Chiya's answer was to take Chananiah by the hand, lead him to the yeshivah, and seat him, as the youth had requested, in a corner, apart from the students.

While Reb Chiya was expounding a passage of the Torah he cast an occasional glance at Chananiah and saw that the youth sat with eyes closed and ears attentive, his face flushing with happiness when the meaning of a word became clear to him and paling with anguish when he failed to understand. Sometimes a pall of fear would descend upon him: he could not make out even a word in translation. To Reb Chiya he seemed like a bewildered creature, lost and stumbling in the desert, parched with thirst yet brightening with hope at the sound of distant water.

Reb Chiya would frequently overhear his students whispering among themselves about Chananiah, taking his name in slander and contempt, and though this brought sadness to his heart he did not rebuke them, for he also saw that Chananiah returned their glances of evil with glances of love, as if they were bestowing a great favor upon him. And so Reb Chiya continued to speak of the Torah.

After Reb Chiya spoke, the students would ask questions and he would answer them. Only Chananiah remained mute, not a word of assent or denial passing his lips. But the devotion—a devotion without end—that he gave to every word glowed upon his face. When the class was done Chananiah would be the last to leave, and, still a solitary, he would spend his afternoon hours walking along the most distant and neglected path, which led to an abandoned hut amidst oleander trees. And there he would sit, lost in meditation, until the time for prayer.

Once, at prayer time, Reb Chiya went to the hut where Chananiah sat and inquired as to the progress Chananiah had made in his studies.

"My knowledge," answered Chananiah, "has yet to be restored to me, but now I do hear the words and I hear them with increasing clarity, and sometimes I can even remember their meanings in translation."

Reb Chiya sighed and remained silent.

"Rabbi," begged Chananiah, "you once used the word *yeshina*—let him tell another. This word has lived in my memory, lighting up the darkness of my soul. Let me speak to you!"

"Of course," said Reb Chiya.

"Sitting alone in this hut, I sometimes surrender myself to meditation, and it seems to me at times that I have been like a cage, full of songbirds that sang God's glory and celebrated His Sabbath. But then there came a magician who cast a spell upon the birds, and they began to sing other melodies, melodies insolent and dissolute. The mob did not understand this and praised both the cage and the birds in the cage, until there once passed through a learned man who paused to listen. He quickly caught the true drift of the melody, the undertones of error and deceit, and he went to the birds and said, 'Rather than sing as you do, may you be stricken dumb!' He blew a harsh blast of cold and angry air into the cage; and then, as if by a miracle, the birds were silent. They fell to the bottom of the cage as if they were frozen, and there they still lie with wings folded, beaks closed, and eyes shut, like the dead.

"And now, when I listen to your discourse and snatch a meaning from one or another word, each of your words seems to waken in me another bird. It opens its little eyes and its mouth and it begins to sing with a soft voice, a quiet voice, but the melodies are good, pious, and truthful melodies, and its wings begin to stir. Soon, soon it will fly."

"You see," comforted Reb Chiya, "God has mercy."

But Chananiah would not be comforted. "All this happens during the day. As soon as the sun goes down, the shadows of night settle again upon my soul. The cage is silent and frozen, the birds that have stirred their wings are lamed once more, and they fall as if dead, with their mouths closed and their eyes shut."

Reb Chiya, from his sadness, could only say, "Go, my son, to the prayers. I shall remain here and pray for you."

Gazing upon Reb Chiya with love and gratitude, Chananiah left.

Reb Chiya remained alone, reciting the evening prayers. As he was leaving the hut, intending to offer a prayer for Chananiah in the open, he saw two snakes twined about oleander trees, with their mouths drooping toward each other so that their venomous tongues almost met.

Reb Chiya was familiar with all the creatures of his garden, those that fly into the heavens, those that slumber on the branches of trees, and those that crawl on the ground. One of the snakes he quickly recognized, but the other, of the species called Achnai, seemed a stranger. But even as he grew curious as to why this snake had come to his garden, he overheard the familiar one ask the visitor this very question.

"I have come to sting someone."

The familiar snake smiled. "Your troubles are in vain. It is many years since I settled here, and when I came I too was a fiery and venomous snake. Frequently would I sting the students of the yeshivah. But with time I ceased. And do you know why? Because Reb Chiya, who is the head of the yeshivah, was once a merchant who traveled over the length and breadth of the world, and from the wise old sheiks whom he met in the deserts he learned many arts, not least of all the art of healing. I would sting and then he would apply the herbs that cured the stings. So I realized that my efforts were being wasted and I simply ceased working."

"Foolishness!" sneered the visiting snake. "Reb Chiya's herbs help only when a snake bites from innate malice, because of the ancient enmity between man and snake. It is well known that the Creator of the Universe prepares a cure for each plague when the plague is not yet visited, and even before he created the venom of snakes he had decreed that the earth should yield its remedies. But I do not fear this, for I come not of my own will, and I shall sting not from the animosity of the snake. I come rather as the servant of the Angel of Death, and I come to carry out a sentence against a man who has been condemned."

"How is that possible?" asked the familiar snake with wonderment. "Here there are only the learned and pious students of Reb Chiya."

"It is Chananiah for whom I come, the youth who meditates here each day."

"But why?"

"This youth once publicly shamed a pupil of Elijah the Prophet. For that sin he was cursed by the head of the Jerusalem yeshivah with the curse of forgetfulness, and it was further decreed that he wander in exile, clad in sackcloth and with an almond staff in hand. Not till the staff blossoms can he again remember the Torah."

"That means—never."

"Who can know?" answered the stranger. "In heaven this sentence was found unsatisfactory; some said it was too mild and declared that Chananiah should be deprived of his share of eternal life. But the Master of the Torah was obdurate; he insisted that the youth be permitted to atone for his sins. A compromise was reached. The youth was to marry a pious daughter of Israel on the eighth day after the wedding he would die. Half of his sin would be atoned for by the blessings of marriage, and the other other half by his death. And since the young woman would be left a widow so quickly, she would be blessed with a son who would become a light of wisdom and a comfort to the world."

The snake grew weary of discourse, never before, perhaps, having spoken at such length. He begged his companion to lead him to water, whereupon the two snakes uncoiled from the trees and glided away. Reb Chiya remained standing, struck with fear.

For Reb Chiya now found himself in a terrible dilemma. If he did nothing to further the marriage of Chananiah, he would be contesting the will of paradise and Chananiah would never recover the Torah. If he helped Chananiah to marry, he would be destroying the youth with his own hands and would, furthermore, be helping to condemn a Jewish daughter to early widowhood.

Reb Chiya searched the heavens; and the heavens kept silent. But his heart began to pound, and a voice within him said, "Chiya, sacrifice thy only daughter Miriam. Father Abraham would not have hesitated."

But it is not so easy to give up one's only daughter. And at this moment Reb Chiya remembered that his sainted wife Sarah had promised that, when need be, she would appear to him in a dream, and so he raised his eyes imploringly. As he prayed, the clouds vanished from his sight and millions of stars came out, promising him that all would yet be well.

His prayer was soon heeded. Once, toward the end of a fast day, Reb Chiya grew faint; his eyes began to close and he fell asleep. In his dream he saw his beloved Sarah, her eyes still shining with the love she had always borne him. As she placed her hand on his right shoulder, she said to him, "Fear not, Chiya. The life of our daughter shall be as bright as the light of the sun. Have faith."

He would have asked her more, but Sarah faded from his dream, and he felt himself being awakened. As Reb Chiya opened his eyes he saw before him his daughter Miriam, her hand on his right shoulder. "Forgive me, Father," she said, "but the sun has long since set, the moon has come into sight, and the stars are shining. It is time for you to break your fast."

Reb Chiya, seeing before him the climax of his dream, took her lovingly by the hand, drew her to his heart, and said, "I shall not break my fast, my daughter, until I have asked you and you have spoken the truth."

And when he saw the color spread across his daughter's face, he said, "My daughter, it is the custom that a young girl should unburden her feelings only to her mother. But you are an orphan, and I must be to you both mother and father. Therefore speak to me in honesty and leave nothing hidden in your heart."

Miriam buried her face in his breast and whispered, "Ask, my father."

"You see that the years pass by and I grow no younger. My beard has become as white as the snows of Mount Hebron. And how shall it be when I am called to my judgment? With whom shall I leave you?"

"Speak not of this, my father. I shall always heed you."

And so he asked, "Would you wish, my daughter, to be more righteous than Rebecca?"

"Not at all." She smiled.

"When Eliezer, the servant of Abraham, came to propose the marriage between Isaac and Rebecca, the Bible says that he was met with the words. 'We shall inquire of her wishes.' Nor was she shamefaced, for she answered, 'Yes, I do.' "

"Ask, father, and I too shall answer."

"Tell me truthfully, which among my students would you desire as a husband?"

"Chananiah," answered Miriam softly, so softly that only a father's ear could have heard the name.

Amazed at the answer, Reb Chiya asked again, "And why does he please you above all others? Have you ever spoken with him?"

"God forbid," she replied. "And besides—would he have answered me?"

Reb Chiya smiled. "What is it then? Tell me." And when he saw that she found it difficult to speak he added, "I command it of you, Miriam, by my right of fatherhood."

And then it was that she told him why Chananiah pleased her above all others, and pleased her from the very first moment. "It was his voice, which flows into my heart with sweetness; and then—it was his strength."

"His strength?" wondered Reb Chiya.

"Surely it shows strength for a youth to go about in sackcloth among the well-clad students and to feel neither shame nor fear."

"And anything else?"

"And for the goodness of his heart, which glows from his eyes whenever he lifts them from the ground. And for his sadness——"

"But he is a penitent, a great sin burdens his soul."

"God will forgive him. He must forgive him!" she cried out. "There have been times when I passed his hut and heard his prayers. Is it conceivable that such heart-rending prayers will not be answered?"

"Our God, Miriam, is a God of Mercy."

"Of his sin I know not, but his atonement is deep. So much regret, so much pain, are cut into his face, and sometimes so much melancholy. One must pity him."

"Is it only pity that you feel?"

"At the beginning that was all. I used to think that if I were you I would constantly pray for him. Afterward the thought came to me: were I his brother I would surrender my life in his behalf. And then—you have asked me to be truthful—a warm stream of blood would rush into my heart. It seemed to me that the deepest sacrifice is possible only to a wife. Since you have commanded me, I speak.

"And once it happened, dear Father, I dreamed—it was on the holiday that you and your pupils went sailing. Chananiah also went—you asked him to—and I, watching through the window, saw the sadness on his face as he followed you. I remained alone in the house—it seemed so sad and lonely. I went into the garden. There too it was quiet; not a bird sang. And I became strangely weary. I looked at the flowers, and they too were drooping. The day was hot; I lay down near the white lilies, my hands folded beneath my head, and gazed at the sky. I slept and I dreamed.

"I dreamed that a dove was flying through the air, so white and gentle and sad. Beneath the dove there flew a black bird of prey, with a sharp beak that sought to stab it. My heart filled with pity for the dove, and I cried out in warning. The dove did not hear me, it continued to fly, but the black bird heard me and, for a moment, made off in alarm. Soon it came back, flying still faster and coming closer to the dove. I felt myself overcome with pity, and I cried still more loudly. Again the black bird grew frightened and turned aside, and again it returned to the chase. This happened several times, until the dove heard me and glided down to ask in tones of sadness, 'Why do you cry, child?' I answered,

'There is a black bird chasing you but you do not see it, and I am trying to frighten it away.' The dove said mournfully, 'It does not *want* to kill me; it *must* kill me. I am condemned to death, and the black bird will carry out the sentence unless someone sacrifices his life for me. And who will do that?' 'I will do it,' I cried to the dove. 'And you will feel no regret?' he asked. 'No, I swear it, I shall never regret.' The dove made signs of affection, stayed for a few moments, and then flew away. And when I awoke I understood what the dream had meant. I knew that the dove was he—Chananiah. I knew that true devotion, devotion without end, can be shown only by a wife. I have sworn, Father, I have sworn!"

Reb Chiya listened, and then he sadly asked, "And how would it be, my daughter, if Chananiah were destined to die in his youth? If he were destined to beget a son who would become a great scholar, but he himself were to leave this world at an early age?"

"Whatever the number of years decreed to him, they shall be happy."

Once more Reb Chiya's eyes grew sad, and again he asked, "And how shall it be if Chananiah is destined to bring forth a great scholar—a truly great one—but his life is reckoned not in years but, from the moment of his wedding, in days?"

"Days then, but days of happiness."

"And you would become a widow in your youth?"

"A widow, but a widow blessed by God."

Reb Chiya remained silent, unable to fathom the strength of his child. A deed of heaven, he thought.

Once again Miriam placed her hand on his shoulder. With eyes uplifted and in a voice that seemed prophetic she said, "I live in the hope that the sentence that hangs over him will be removed. I shall offer my life for his."

"But how, my daughter?"

"I do not know, since the sin for which he suffers is unknown to me. Later he will tell me."

In Reb Chiya's heart there could remain no doubt that this was a destined marriage. God tries me, he thought, and I shall endure the trial. To his daughter he said, "*Mazel tov*, my child. With God's blessing, we will arrange the betrothal tomorrow."

Miriam bent to kiss her father's hand, and when she rose Reb Chiya could hardly recognize her, so transported had her face become with happiness and joy.

"You have no fear, Miriam?"

"No, I wait upon God's word." Her voice rang as clear and pure as crystal.

But after Miriam left, Reb Chiya could not quiet his fears and he dispatched letters to the head of the yeshivah in Jerusalem and to the head of the Jews in Babylon. To them he poured out all his woe and perplexity.

"Tomorrow we shall mark the betrothal of my daughter Miriam, may God grant her long life. There are moments when it seems that I am placing a crown upon her head, and moments when I feel that I am leading my only child, my little white lamb, to the slaughter. Yet I do not wish to oppose the will of God. I shall set the date of the wedding for a month from this day, and during this month I shall wait for word from you, for your counsel and your wisdom. And I beg you to pray for me, to pray for my daughter and for the penitent youth as well."

The next day the betrothal took place. Everyone gasped, and the students of the yeshivah were beside themselves with astonishment. That such good fortune should befall Chananiah! But out of respect for their teacher they said not a word.

So the month passed. No letter for Reb Chiya came from Jerusalem or Babylon, which seemed to him an evil omen. On the day of the wedding he drew Miriam aside and said to her, "Do you know, my child, that your beloved Chananiah is fated to leave this world on the eighth day after the wedding?" And then he repeated what the snake had said and told her that he had not yet heard from Jerusalem and Babylon. If there was a speck of uncertainty in her heart, she could still withdraw.

Miriam replied "I am certain, and my heart is certain. Now that I know the sentence I know how to undo it."

"You! By what virtues and by what powers?" wondered Reb Chiya.

"By the power of my faith, and by the virtue of my mother, may she rest with God, and of you, my father."

The wedding canopy was made ready.

The bridegroom came in his sackcloth, with a hempen rope about his loins and in his hands a staff made from a peeled almond branch. Since he could not speak, Reb Chiya delivered the wedding sermon for him, and Chananiah listened with joy and with sorrow.

And when the bridegroom was led to his bride, she awaited him in workday clothes, with a drab kerchief covering her hair, so that she would not place herself above him.

And when the time came for the bride to be unveiled, her face shone like the sun and her eyes were clear and trusting and quiet, yet happy beyond measure.

And the bride was led around the bridegroom seven times, dressed as she was in her workday clothes, so as not to burden the heart of her beloved. Reb Chiya watched, with pride and with tears.

When Chananiah was asked to repeat the Hebrew words of the marriage ceremony he asked, "What do the words mean?"

Reb Chiya translated from the Hebrew, word for word.

All Safed gasped. And they gasped still more when the groom spoke not a word of Torah at the wedding feast.

The ceremony of the Seven Blessings that followed the wedding was held in the garden. The bride sat among the women like an orphan among the wealthy, and the groom like a dullard among scholars and rabbis discoursing upon Torah. Reb Chiya, no matter whether he spoke himself or listened to others, sat nervous and ill at ease, his eyes searching through the garden. Not that he regretted the wedding! He was, rather, looking for the strange snake, and soon he saw how Achnai glided silently among the guests, seen by none of them, never taking his eyes off its victim, the youth Chananiah.

On the evening of the seventh day of the Seven Blessings, Reb Chiya drew his daughter to his side and in a strained voice said to her, "Tomorrow is the day of judgment. Be strong, my daughter!"

"I am strong," replied the young wife, "for I am blessed by God. And I will redeem my husband from death."

"God be with you," said Reb Chiya, his eyes filling with hot tears.

"But remember," added Miriam, "tomorrow the miracle must occur. The staff must bloom and so must his soul! He must recite to you a portion of the Torah! Come to us early, dear Father."

The next morning, when Reb Chiya came to them, Miriam was already dressed but Chananiah still lay in bed. "Forgive me," he said to his father-in-law, closing his eyes, "I do not feel well."

Reb Chiya, however, was staring at the white staff that stood by Chananiah's bed. For the staff was slowly turning green, veins were beginning to course through it and tiny blossoms to appear. As Reb Chiya drew closer to gaze upon this miracle, he saw that Chananiah's face was also undergoing a transformation. Slowly it took on color, and the eyes, when Chananiah opened them, were clear and tranquil, untroubled by any curse. Reb Chiya turned to his daughter, to see whether she too had noticed this miracle, but Miriam was no longer in sight. Soon, however, Reb Chiya forgot his daughter and the miracle of the staff and even the snake Achnai, the messenger of the Angel of Death; for Chananiah had opened his lips and the words had begun to flow. They flowed like pearls of wisdom, wisdom that lighted up the Torah and the inner secrets and mysteries of the Torah. Chananiah, as he spoke, opened for Reb Chiya the gates to a new world, a paradise where the tree of knowledge and the tree of life and many other marvelous trees were blossoming. The clear light of the first seven days shone upon this paradise as with rays of gold; among the leaves sang a multitude of birds, and on every side there was a blossoming and burgeoning of life. Chananiah spoke; and to Reb Chiya it seemed that the soul of the world was speaking. Straining ears and eyes, Reb Chiya drank in every word that streamed from Chananiah's lips, and a great bliss, silent and holy, spread through his whole being.

The secrets and the mysteries of the Torah, as Chananiah unfolded them to Reb Chiya, were later recorded in the Book of Chananiah, which Reb Chiya issued with bindings of gold. But since these are wonders not to be described, let us leave the sages of the Torah and turn to the blessed Miriam.

Once she had seen her father gazing upon the miracle of the staff, Miriam snatched up her husband's sackcloth and ran from the room. Quietly and lightly she went through the palace, the thick carpet muffling her steps, and once alone she quickly threw off her clothes. "Forgive me, my God," she murmured, "forgive me if I violate the law that forbids a woman to wear the dress of a man, but a life is at stake." And she lowered Chananiah's sackcloth over her body and ran into the garden. She remained there quietly, staring at the path that wound its way from the door of the house far, far into the distance, until it disappeared among the oleander trees.

Murmuring prayers to the Almighty that he accept her sacrifice, Miriam saw the messenger of the Angel of Death, Achnai, uncoil itself from an oleander tree, and she quickly covered her face with her hands so as to seem to it like the fated victim Chananiah. Between the cracks of her fingers she watched the snake approach her, gliding slowly and with assurance, for it knew that its victim could not flee.

When the snake saw Chananiah (as it supposed) sitting calmly, waiting with his face covered, it thought: My victim waits and his heart is filled with foreboding. He is praying or perhaps confessing. The snake uncovered its fangs of venom. Miriam saw how Achnai began to move faster, now that its appetite was aroused. She heard the rustle of its skin over the ground. And when it had come so close that she could see the spots on its skin, Miriam closed her fingers and prayed silently in her heart, Lord of the Universe, accept my sacrifice! Quietly, without taking breath, she began her last confession, and not once did her lips tremble. Before the prayer was done she felt the sting of the fangs—and fell to the ground with the cry, "O Lord of the Universe, forgive me for the great scholar with which you were to bless me. May Chananiah live in his place!"

The death struggle followed, and it was with great pain that the soul tore its way out of her body.

But our God is a God of Judgment.

When Miriam's soul rose to heaven, the saints of paradise were waiting for it, or more exactly, they were waiting for the soul of Chananiah. And when she was led to the seat of judgment she was asked, merely for the sake of custom, since the answer was known to all, "Were your dealings on earth honest?"

Answered Miriam, "I had no dealings on earth."

"Did you study the Torah?"

She smiled charmingly. "Lord of the Universe, have you ever directed the daughters of Israel to study your Torah?"

A tumult broke out. "Who are you? Who are you?"

"Miriam, daughter of Sarah and Chiya, wife of Chananiah!"

Consternation! The heavenly host realized that she had sacrificed herself, from devotion without end, for her husband, and that Achnai, the messenger of the Angel of Death, had been deceived.

So they cried out to her soul, "Return, quickly! Return to your body before it is moved."

No, said Miriam, and refused. To suffer twice the agonies of death, she declared, is beyond the burden placed on man. Unless, of course, she said, they would accept her death in place of Chananiah's. For he must live.

"Agreed, agreed!" rose the cry in heaven. They were fearful of delay.

And at that very moment Miriam's soul returned to her body, and she rose from the ground without even a wound. With great joy she ran to tell her husband and her father what had happened, and as she entered the palace there arrived two messengers, one from the head of the yeshivah of Jerusalem and the other other from the head of the Jews of Babylon. Both letters said only: "*Mazel tov!*"

About the great scholar that was born to Miriam, and of the satisfaction he brought to Reb Chiya, we may, with God's help, speak another time. Here it need only be added that the snake Achnai, the messenger of the Angel of Death who had let himself be deceived, was promptly dismissed and has never been heard from since.

Translated by Irving Howe and Eliezer Greenberg

A Musician Dies

A skeleton lies in bed, a skeleton covered with yellow, thin, dry skin. Mikhel, the musician, is dying. Mirrel, his wife, sits near him on a chest, her eyes swollen with crying. Their eight sons, all musicians, are spread around the crowded room. Silence. No one speaks to any of the others. The doctor has given up on Mikhel. So has the barber.

There will be nothing to inherit. The local Burial Society will donate his shroud and the grave. The Society of Pallbearers will add a little brandy. Nothing more to say; all is clear and definite. Only Mirrel refuses to concede. After everything seemed settled, she began to create a tumult in the synagogue. She has just come from incantations in the graveyard. Now, she keeps insisting, "He is dying because the children are sinful. They aren't pious. They carouse. That is why God is taking their father. The band of musicians is losing its glory. No wedding will be the way it ought to. No Jew will have a true festivity."

God's compassion is great. One must shout, entreat, do something that will move Him. But they, the children, they have no pity. They do not wear the ritual undergarment. Oh, if only it weren't for their sins! She has an uncle—a *shokhet*—in heaven. He must be in the top rank. He would not refuse her. When he was living—may his memory be blessed—he would always pet her. Even now, he probably is well-disposed. No doubt, he made an effort; he did everything he could. But the sins, the sins!

"They ride to Gentile dances. Eat Gentile bread and butter. God knows what else they eat there! They don't wear the undergarments. Her uncle is trying. But he won't be able to succeed. Oh, the sins, the sins!"

The sons do not answer. They stare at the floor, each in his corner.

"There is still time," she whimpers. "Children! Hurry and do penance."

"Mirrel," the invalid cries. "Let be. It's no use, Mirrel, I am done for. Mirrel, I want to die."

She begins to flare up: "A nice state of affairs. Die. He wants to die. And me? What of me? No! I will not let you. You must live. You must. I'll make such a scene the spirit won't be able to leave you." An unhealed wound has apparently opened in her heart.

"Mirrel, let be!" the invalid pleads. "We cursed each other enough when I was alive. Enough! It's not proper when I'm dying. Oh, Mirrel. I have sinned. You too have sinned. It is enough. Let us be silent. I keep feeling how the coldness of death is creeping up along my body from my toes to my heart. Inch by inch, Mirrel, I am dying. Do not scream. It is better this way."

"Because you want to get rid of me," Mirrel interrupts. "That's what you always wanted," she cries bitterly. "Always! You had dark Peshke in your heart. You would always say that you want to die. Oh, misery! Even now he doesn't repent. Even now—now!"

He smiles a bit sadly. "Not only dark Peshke. There were lots of dark ones, fair ones, and some were red-headed. But, Mirrel, I never wanted to be rid of you! A woman is a woman. That's how it is with musicians. It's remarkable! It draws like a blister. But a wife is a wife! These are two different things. Remember, how when Peshke said something bad about you, I gave her a going over, right there in the middle of the street.

"So hush. Be quiet! A wife is a wife. Unless there is a divorce. My heart will be aching. Mirrel, believe me. I will be longing for you. You, too, my sons. You too have given me enough trouble. But it doesn't matter. As we musicians say, it has all gone into the fiddle. I know, you liked me, but you didn't really respect me. If I took an extra drop of brandy, you would grumble I was a drunkard. It is not right. It is improper to treat a father this way. Still, I had a father and I didn't treat him any better. Enough of that—I forgive you."

He grew tired.

After a few seconds, "I forgive you," he continued. Then, raising his body slightly, he regarded the others.

"Look at them," he suddenly cried. "Oxen. Their eyes screwed into the ground. Can't even count to two. After all, a father is a loss! Even if a drunkard. Eh?"

The youngest raised his eyes and his lashes trembled. He began to cry. The brothers followed. In a minute, the tiny room was full of lamentations.

The invalid watched—delighted.

"Well," he said suddenly with a new vigor. "Enough. I'm afraid it will make me feel too sorry. Enough. Obey your father."

"You heartless man! Let them cry," Mirrel shouted. "Their tears may help you."

"Mirrel, be silent. I've already told you. I have played my piece. Enough! Hayim, Berl . . . Yonah. All of you. Listen! Hurry! Take up your instruments."

All stared. "I order. I beg you. Please me," said the invalid. "Take your instruments and come close to the bed."

The sons obeyed; they surrounded the bed. Three fiddles, a clarinet, a bass horn, a trumpet.

"Let me hear," the sick man said, "how the band will play without me. Mirrele, please. Ask the neighbor to come in."

The neighbor was the *shammes* of the Pallbearers Society. At first, Mirrel didn't want to go; but he looked at her so pleadingly that she had to obey. Afterward, she used to say that the word "Mirrele" and the look he gave her just before his death were the same as those right after they got married. She would say, "Do you remember, children, his tender voice and eyes?"

The *shammes* came in. His eyes looked up and down. "Forgive me, Mirrel," he said. "Call in a *minyan*."

"Don't need 'em," said the invalid. "Why would I need a *minyan*? I have my own: my band of musicians. Mirrel, don't go. I don't need a *minyan*."

Turning his body to them, "Listen, children," he said. "Play without me as you played when I was here. Play right; don't clown at a poor man's wedding. . . . Be respectful to your mother. And now—play my act of confession! The neighbor will recite the words."

And the little house became full of music!

Translated by Nathan Halper

Venus and Shulamith

In a little prayer house two young yeshivah students, Hayim and Selig, were seated by the stove. Hayim was reading aloud from Selig's notebook and Selig was listening while mending his shoe with a needle and thread.

" '. . . And beautiful was Hannah like Venus . . .' Tell me, Selig, please, what does this word *Venus* mean?" asked Hayim.

"Venus is a mythological goddess," answered Selig, driving the needle into the shoe.

"Mythology? What's all that?"

"You know nothing about that either? Think back a little: remember the strange looking man who appeared a week ago wearing an apron and a red cap, the one who sold licorice cookies and other such things for practically nothing?"

"Yes, so?"

"He was a Greek and there is a whole group of people called Greeks."

"And they all sell licorice cookies?"

"Don't be silly, they have their own land: Greece. They are an ancient people, mentioned in the Bible. Their land is called in Hebrew *Iavan* and they are called *Ivanim.*"

"What? *Iavan?* And from this comes *Ivan* in the Russian?"

"God forbid! Greeks are Greeks, with their own kingdom. They once were a very strong and learned people. I'm sure you've heard of Aristotle and Socrates. Our talmudic sages and even Maimonides knew about them. Aristotle, for example, believed the world was created out of chaos. Such were the Greeks. And even though they were very learned and knew how to paint, sculpt, carve, and appreciate fine things, they were nothing but idol worshippers serving false gods."

"How sad!"

"So you see, the stories and tales of the gods, of the idols, are called mythology."

"Well then, what is Venus?"

"Understand that with the Greeks each trade and each craft had its own god. Just as we say that each people has its own genius, such as sculpture, poetry, beauty, health, prowess . . ."

"And they all have gods? Then what do you mean by *goddess*? A little god?"

"No. A god is a 'he' and a goddess is a 'she.' "

"What? They allowed unmarried women to roam about in heaven?"

"Oh, Hayim, why only men and not women?"

"It's true, Selig, but I thought that gods should be neither male nor female."

"Hayim, you must understand that Greek gods are just like humans, with the difference that they are immortal. Therefore they have children, wives, and mistresses just like us, only they never die! Even Jupiter, the greatest of their gods, who holds thunder in his hands and makes all the other gods tremble with fright, even he is only a henpecked husband. To his wife, Juno, he's like a little Hebrew teacher snubbed by the rabbi's wife. I told you once about the philosopher Socrates' wife, Xanthippe, the shrew. Why, she was small fry compared to Juno! If you could imagine how Jupiter suffered at her hands! At least ten times a day he wished he was dead. But it's impossible, he can never die."

"I get the point. And Venus?"

"Venus is the goddess of beauty. Now I'll read to you about her life."

Selig put aside the half-mended shoe, drew out a soiled piece of paper from his breast pocket and began to read from it.

" 'Venus, Aphrodite, Apogenena, Pontogenea, Andiametha . . .' "

"I don't understand a word you are saying," said Hayim, bewildered.

"Little fool. Those are the names by which Venus was known in the various parts of Greece and later in Rome."

"She has more names than Adam. What's the use of all these names? Get to the story."

Selig continued reading: " 'Under her many appellations, she was held sacred as the goddess of love in various towns and cities.' "

"No longer of beauty?"

"It's all the same! 'She was not born of a mother but sprang forth from the sea. She is the ideal image of womanhood and very alluring as well.' "

"*Alluring?* What does that mean?"

"It means she knows how to entice everyone, excite them, and get them hot, etc."

"I see!"

" 'She was represented as either scantily dressed or entirely naked.' "

"That doesn't sound so good."

" 'Her husband was Vulcan.' "

"What manner of beast is that?"

"Another god, a god of fire similar to Tubal-Cain. He invented the forging of iron and founded the blacksmith's trade. Understand?"

"A little . . ."

" 'But she had no children by him.' Gods do not divorce or marry according to the laws of holy matrimony. 'Therefore she had children by other gods and even by mortals.' "

"Just like that? Do you know what they call such children? Bastards, that's what they're called!"

"Don't be a fool, Hayim! Gods are not bound by the laws of marriage, sanctity, or divorce. They have no shame about sexual things or having bastards."

"Of course, if you don't accept the laws, why pay them lip service? If you don't wash your hands, why say the blessings? But you said she lay with mortals too?"

"Well, what about it? Didn't some of our own saintly men, mentioned in Scriptures, go in for . . ."

"Read on, read on!"

" 'She had two children by Mars . . .' "

"Morris was involved?"

"No, not Morris, *Mars*, the god Mars, the god of war! 'Two by Bacchus, the god who oversees the making of wine and other spirits.' "

"He must be like Lot, a real drunk."

" 'Two by Mercury . . .' "

"And who is he?"

"Mercury is the god of swindlers, traders, and messengers."

"Quite an unsavory pair."

" 'And one by Anchises, a mortal whom Venus, disguised as a shepherdess, happened to meet near a river. A child was born from that encounter. Once the following incident took place. A band of cutthroats chased Venus. She took refuge in a cave and called for Hercules.' "

"Who?"

"A powerful god, not quite a full god but only a demi-god. All by himself, he cleaned out thirty-six stalls in a stable."

"Get to the point, Selig, this is becoming irritating and a little confusing."

" 'Hercules came into the cave and let each cutthroat enter one by one. He showed the way to each.' "

"How disgusting!"

" 'Venus used to take revenge on people who spurned love. She metamorphosed townspeople into oxen.' "

"Enough," blurted Hayim, jumping out of his chair. "Enough! I'm absolutely sick. This you call a goddess! And she had a thousand men massacred, run through, and slaughtered! And she gives herself to adultery, whoring, and murder! It's sickening!"

Hayim spat and Selig stood foaming with rage.

"Do you know what you are saying and spitting at?" Selig shouted. "You are taking a nice garment, turning it inside out and making it into a clown's outfit. I only used Venus as a comparison, an ideal figure in a particular setting as, for instance, Shulamith in the Song of Songs."

"And that is an accurate comparison? Really! You should be ashamed of yourself, Selig. As if they were alike! Her brothers called her into their vineyards, but she did not keep her own vineyard. Her face is swarthy but not like a gypsy. Her neck is like fine marble. She smells sweeter than all the fields, woods, and gardens. She does not glance up from bashfulness and does not swell with pride like a turkey cock. She looks straight ahead and has nothing to be ashamed of. She has fine, warm, and sincere eyes like two pretty doves. And she has lips—two thin, red feathers! She never sneers with her little mouth or makes ugly faces. She speaks openly and honey flows from her mouth. You know very well that she does not make any evil thoughts come into your head; on the contrary, you forget about whatever you were thinking. She casts her eyes upon you and your own turn away like a thief. Your very heart begins to quiver and tremble like a freshly killed hen. She is simple, pure, and clean as the new-fallen snow. As the summer comes forth, so new life returns to the field and the garden. The turtledove begins to coo, the flowers begin to bud, the fig tree blossoms, the grapes sparkle. Everything comes back to life, everything awakens to a new life and her heart knows a new sensation. A new feeling suddenly comes over her with intense power. Stronger than death is her love, deeper than hell is her jealousy; and her love is forever. Rivers cannot carry it off, the sea itself cannot extinguish it. She has but one love, a young, handsome shepherd. She does not know that the shepherd wears a crown on his head, and that he is the greatest king in the world. She is simple, open, and noble. She cannot assume a role, or act fickle. It hurts her that he is not her brother from the same father and mother so that she can kiss him openly and freely on all the streets. Such is Shulamith. She is the ideal of a true Jewish maiden. Not like your Venus, that hussy!"

"You are forgetting one thing," interrupted Selig, "you forget that everything called mythology is just fables that contain hidden philosophic and religious thoughts."

"Oh no, it's you that have the argument backwards. It's just the opposite. How can profound thoughts be clothed in shabby examples? How can one wrap diamonds in dirty rags? And do you think we Jews do not read the Song of Songs as a parable? Isn't Solomon the Almighty Himself? And isn't Shulamith the Jewish people, the innocent but persecuted Jewish people! But why all these hidden meanings? Shulamith is Shulamith and Venus is . . . Why, there are a hundred thousand million differences between them. It's not even worth talking about. Do you hear, Selig! Blot her out! Erase her name from your book and write the name of . . . what's the name of the girl you are describing? Hannah, wasn't it?"

"Hannah."

"Yes, so write that she was a beautiful as. . . . No, don't write anything! You hear? Don't you dare! It would be impudent of you. Let your Hannah be compared to whomever you like: to Miriam with her timbrel, to Abigail, to Rehavah, to Delilah, even to Queen Esther; but not to Shulamith! No one can be compared to her, absolutely no one, you hear?"

Translated by Seth L. Wolitz

The Poor Boy

"Give me five kopecks for a night's flop."

"No," I answer curtly and walk on.

He runs after me, his eyes flaming with a doglike yearning. He grabs my sleeve, kisses it—but no use. "I just can't afford such handouts every day."

These paupers, I tell myself after leaving the soup kitchen where I had been so harsh to the young beggar, these paupers quickly turn out to be a terrible nuisance.

The first time I had seen that haggard young face, with its glittering, melancholy yet clever eyes, I was deeply shaken. Hardly had he opened his mouth than a coin came speeding out of my pocket and into his bony hand.

I remember perfectly well: it seemed as if my hand were acting quite on its own. It never stopped to ask my heart whether if felt pity or my mind whether a man living on an income of forty-one rubles, sixty-six kopecks a month could afford to give five kopecks to a beggar.

The boy's request went though me like an electric spark, flashing into every limb of my body. Only later, when he had skipped happily out of the kitchen, did my mind take into account this new expense.

I was a man laden with worries, my own and those of others, so I soon forgot about the boy. But not, it seems, entirely. Somewhere within me there must have taken place a focusing of my practical instincts. For the next evening, when the boy stopped me again, begging in his choked-up voice for the price of a night's lodging, there swarmed into my mind a cluster of ready-made thoughts: a boy of 7 or 8 should not beg . . . should not hang around the soup kitchen . . . snatching food from dishes before they've been cleared . . . it will only make him into an idler, a little beggar. . . . No good can come of that.

Again my hand started moving of its own accord, but I trapped it in my pocket and stopped it there. Had I been a religious man, I'd have thought: Is this good deed worth the expenditure of five kopecks? Or couldn't I balance out my heavenly account in another way, with some especially fervent signs at evening prayers? But not being pious, I thought only of the boy's own good. The five kopecks would do him nothing but harm, confirming his worst habits as a beggar.

And yet—I gave him the money a second time. My hand seemed eager to fly out of my pocket, I couldn't control it. Something hurt inside me and my eyes grew moist. Again the boy leapt out of the kitchen, and I felt as if a weight had been lifted from my heart. A smile stole across my face.

The third time it took me longer, much longer, to decide. I had already reckoned that my earnings simply weren't enough for me to keep donating five kopecks every day. True, it gave me real pleasure to see this haggard boy jumping up and down with joy, his eyes lighting up, and to know that for a few coins he now wouldn't have to spend the night wandering in the streets but could go to the lodging house where it would be warm and he'd get a glass of tea and a roll in the morning. All this gave me pleasure. But with my income, I concluded, I just couldn't indulge such pleasures.

Not that I said all this to the boy. I preferred to lecture him, of course.

I gave him to understand that begging would ruin him; that everyone—and he too—must grow up a man; that it was the duty of every man to work; that work is sacred and if he really looked, he would find some. I passed along other bits of wisdom that I had gotten out of books: none of which could be a substitute for a night's lodging, or even an umbrella on a rainy night.

He just stood there, hugging my sleeve and raising his eyes to see whether he could find a fleck of pity in my face. I began to feel his hopes weren't in vain. My frigid thoughts started to melt. His doglike pleading eyes were having an effect on me. Again, I'd give in.

And then an idea came to me. Yes, I'd give him the money, but this time I'd tell him he must never beg again. I would speak with such authority, he would never forget it.

I gave him the five kopecks: "Here, take it! And don't you ever beg from me again!"

From me! Where had those words come from? That wasn't

what I had meant at all. I'd gladly have given him a few more kopecks if only I could have taken back those words. A chill went through my soul—it was as if I had ripped off my skin and now I was bare. All this passed, however, in a second or two, and meanwhile the sternness of my look, the admonishing thrust of my hand, the metallic clang of my voice—all made the point. Swaying before me as if on hot coals, yearning to rush away, the boy turned paler and paler as I lectured him. A tear started trembling on his eyelids.

"No more begging," I repeated sternly, "You hear? Let this be the last time!"

The boy caught his breath—and fled.

Today, I really didn't give him anything. I'm not the sort to break my word. I don't make vows lightly, I don't swear by the holy books—with me, my word is my word. A man has to stand by what he says, otherwise there'd be no order in this world. I think over again what I've said and feel satisfied with myself.

I just can't keep handing out five kopecks a day. But that's not the most important thing. The most important thing is that I'm acting for the boy's own good, and for the good of the community too. What's the use of charity if there's no system, and how can you have system without a firm hand?

With the boy I had spoken in plain Yiddish; with myself I spoke in a more learned fashion, using scientific terms. Begging, I reflected, is the most pernicious microbe in the body social. Whoever does not work has no right to live, etc., etc.

No sooner had I closed the door of the soup kitchen than I was swallowed up by the dark night. My feet sank into the mud. The wind was fierce, the flames of the street lamps seemed to tremble with the cold, and their feeble lights reflected in puddles of mud made me dizzy. The wind whistled plaintively, as if a thousand souls were begging for redemption or a thousand boys for five kopecks to pay for a flop.

Damn! That boy again!

You wouldn't drive a dog into the street on a night like this, and yet the boy will have to spend it there. Still, what am I supposed to do? Weren't three times enough? Now, let someone else take care of him! Enough that I, with my cough and my weak throat, trouble to do my share at the soup kitchen. I'm a member of the charity committee, but no one would really expect me out in weather like this—and without a fur coat, too. At least if I were religious, there'd be some ultimate benefit. I'd run home, throw myself into bed and fall asleep; my soul would rise to heaven and make certain that this good deed was entered on the credit side of the ledger. But in fact I had done everything without a thought of personal advantage. I had done it because my heart told me to.

Comforting myself with praise, I began to feel a little better. When it is someone else who praises me, I experience a certain embarrassment and try to brush it away with my hand. But when it's my own praise, I can listen without shame. In fact, I might have continued in this vein, finding more good qualities in myself to praise, had I not stepped deep into the mud with my worn-out shoes. God knows, my frequent visits to the soup kitchen had helped wear them out.

The Talmud says "Whoever goes on an errand of mercy will come to no grief." But it seems that such protection applies only on the way to a good deed, not back from it. Returning full of righteousness, a man can break his neck!

My feet grew wet, the cold seeped into my bones. I felt certain I would catch cold, perhaps I'd already caught one. Soon there'd be that stabbing pain in the chest. I grew frightened. It was only a little while since I'd spent a few weeks in bed.

Surely I've caught cold. I was still a long way from my home and my boots were filling with water. Suddenly I noticed the lighted windows of a cafe, the worst one in Warsaw—dreadful tea. But no matter. I crossed the street, entered a warm lighted room, and ordered a glass of steaming tea.

Paying for the tea that has barely touched my lips, I again remember the beggar boy. He has no umbrella, no home, no bed. But what on earth made me think of him? A thought I could not suppress: that what I had paid for the tea would have been enough for his flop, even a slice of bread and some soup as well.

And why did I order the tea at all? Food would be waiting for me at home, and a pleasant smile too. I had ordered the tea simply because I felt ashamed of going into the cafe without buying something.

Well, I comforted myself, you have to pay for your shame too.

Outside the storm had grown worse. The wind tore into the roofs like an anti-Semite assaulting Jews. The storm lashed at the street lamps, but they remained erect, continuing to shed their light as if martyred scholars in the days of the Inquisition. Plunging deeper, the storm ripped into the very pavement and then, in a new rage, it rose up again, toward the heavens. But the heavens were distant, indifferent. The people who had to be out on the streets were doubled up, their heads lowered, shrinking into themselves, as if to take up as little space as possible while yet continuing on their way.

Again, that poor unhappy boy. How will he manage? My philosophy crumbles; pity takes its place. Were he my child being carried away by this mad wind, would I hesitate a moment?

I lost all desire to go home. It seemed as if I had no right to a comfortable house, hot tea, a warm bed, a smile of welcome. "Murderer" and "Cain" were engraved on my forehead. I did not dare to face my fellow creatures.

Devil take it! If only I were pious, all would be easier. How pleasant it would be to know that He who dwells in the highest heavens never takes His eyes off this world and will never forget the beggar boy for a moment!

Still, why should that boy weigh so heavily on my heart? Why not thrust him onto the heart of the entire world? I wouldn't worry about him at all if I could believe that he lives securely under the eye of the Cosmos. That eye shut for a moment, whole worlds could be seized by the devil; open, it will not allow the smallest worm to perish without being accounted for.

And yet, out of feelings of shame, I turned back to the soup kitchen, not going there directly but twisting and turning through several blocks. Why did I feel shame? To this day I don't know.

The dining room was empty. The turmoil of the day had begun to settle, the vapors from the wet floor were rising to the ceiling. Through a little window I watched the sleepy cook, her wig askew, as she leaned with her left hand on an enormous pot and with her right hand slowly lifted a large spoon to her mouth. The assistant cook was there too, sleepily preparing noodles for the next day. The director was counting the tickets for dinners served by the committee. There was no one else. I glanced under the tables, but not a trace of the boy. Too late.

It's lucky at least, I thought to myself, that no one has seen me here. I left the soup kitchen.

I have been wandering around for hours. What's the matter with me? I grow irritable, angry, and start for home.

Good, everyone is alseep. I take off my shoes at the door, sneak quietly into the house, and creep into bed. But I have a bad night. It is hard to fall asleep, a shudder runs through my bones, and I wake up in a cold sweat. I spring out of bed and stumble toward the window. The wind is still raging, the house seems to tremble.

I go back to bed, no longer hoping to sleep, but doze off a little, troubled by dreams, all about the boy. Each time I see him in a different place. He is trudging along a muddy street, crouching on some stairs under the roof of a shop, being tossed like a ball in mid-air by a pack of demons, lying frozen and stiff on a dunghill.

I can hardly wait until morning. I run straight to the soup kitchen.

There he is!

If I weren't ashamed, I'd wash the dirt from his face with my grateful tears; if I weren't fearful of my wife, I'd take him home.

I am not a murderer!

"Here," I handed him a ten kopeck piece. He looks at me with astonishment, unaware of what he has done for me.

The next day I give him nothing. But at least I don't preach. And what is more, I feel ashamed and dissatisfied with myself.

Not for nothing did my grandfather, God rest his soul, keep saying to me, "The unbeliever lives a life of heartache and dies without comfort."

Translated and abridged by Irving Howe and Eliezer Greenberg

Travel Pictures*

My first halting place was Tishevitz. I took lodgings with an acquaintance, Reb Boruch. He sent for the beadle and a few householders.

While I was waiting for them I stood by the window and looked out at the marketplace. It was a large square bounded on every side by a row of grimy, tumble-down houses, some roofed with straw, but the majority with shingle. All were one-storied and had broad porches supported by rotting beams.

Out in front of the porches, and with not too much room between them, stood huckstresses over stalls holding rolls, bread, peas, beans, and various kinds of fruit. The marketwomen are in a state of great commotion. I must have made a big impression on them.

"Bad luck to you!" screams one. "Don't point at him with your finger; he can see!"

"Hold your tongue!"

The women know that I have come to take down things in writing. They confide the secret to one another so softly that I overhear every word, even inside the house.

"They say it is *he* [Satan] himself!"

"It is a good thing the poor sheep have shepherds watching over them. All the same, if *that* shepherd didn't help, much good it would do!"

---

*Early in his career, before he had found his voice as a writer, Peretz undertook a journey through the small Jewish towns of Poland, collecting data for a projected census and meanwhile noting his impressions of Jewish life. The result was a book called *Pictures of a Provincial Journey*, sketches often notable for their sharp and poignant ironies. We print here a few selections from this book, as translated in *Stories and Pictures*, a volume of Peretz writings first published by the Jewish Publication Society of America.

"A person can't understand why *that* shepherd should require such messengers" (an allusion to my shaven face and short-skirted coat). . . .

I began with my host. He has no wife, and before I could put in a word he excused himself for it by asking, "How long do you suppose she's been dead?"—lest I should reproach him for not having found another to fill her place.

Well, to be brief, I set him down a widower, three sons married, one daughter married, two little boys and one little girl at home. And here he begs me at once to put down that all his sons—except the youngest, who is only four years old, "and the Messiah will come before *he* is liable for military service"—are exempt from serving for one reason or another.

With the exception of the two eldest sons, I already know the whole family.

The married daughter lives in her father's house and sells tobacco, snuff, tea, and sugar; also foodstuffs; also I think, kerosene and grease. I had bought some sugar from her early that morning. She is about twenty-eight years old. A thin face, a long hooked nose that seems to be trying to count the black and decaying teeth in her half-opened mouth, cracked, blue-gray lips—the image of her father. Her sister, a young girl, is like her but she has *kalla-kheyn*, maidenly charm, her face is fresher and pinker, her teeth whiter, and altogether she is not so worn and neglected looking. I also see the two little boys, pretty little boys, they must take after their mother: red cheeks, and shy, restless eyes, their tight black curls full of feathers. But they have ugly habits, are always shrugging their little shoulders and writhing peevishly. They wear quilted coats, dirty but in one piece.

The mother can't have died more than a short time ago, long enough for the coats to get dirty, not long enough for them to get torn. Who is there to look after them now? The eldest sister has four children, a husband who is a scholar, and the shop—the little *kalla* maiden waits on her father's customers at the bar: the father himself has no time.

"What business are you in?" I ask him.

"Percentage."

"Do you mean usury?"

"Well, call it usury if you want to. It doesn't amount to anything either way. Do you know what?" he exclaims. "Take all my rubbish and welcome, bills of exchange, deeds—everything for 25 percent, only pay me in cash. I'll give up usury, even the public house! God knows how I'd love to go to Palestine—but give me the cash! Take the whole business and welcome! You think we live on usury—it lives on us! People don't pay up, the debt grows bigger. The bigger it gets, the less it's worth, and the poorer I am, I give you my word!"

Before going out to take further notes, I witness a little scene. While I was gathering up my things, paper, pencil, cigarettes, Reb Boruch was buttering bread for the children to take with them to *heder*. They each had two slices of bread and butter and a tiny onion as a relish.

"Now go!" he says; he does not want them in the public house. But the little orphan isn't satisfied. He hunches his shoulders and pulls a wry face preparatory to crying. He feels a bit ashamed, however, to cry in front of me, and waits till I am gone. But he can't wait so long and lets out a wail.

"Another little onion!" he wants. "Mother always gave *me* two!"

The sister has come running into the taproom and catches up another onion and gives it to him. "Go!" she says also, but much more gently.

The mother's voice sounded in her words.

We go from house to house, from number to number. I can see for myself which houses are inhabited by Jews and which by Gentiles; I have only to look at the windows. Dingy windows are a sure sign of "Thou hast chosen us," still more so broken panes stuffed with cushions and sacking. On the other hand, flower pots and curtains show the presence of those who have no such right to poverty as the others.

One meets with exceptions—here lives, *not* a Jew, but a drunkard—and here again, flowers and curtains, but they read *Hatzefirah*. [A Hebrew newspaper, to subscribe to which meant that one was "enlightened" and "advanced."] . . . And don't imagine Tishevitz is the world's end. It has a *maskil*, too, and a real *maskil*, one of the old style, middle-aged, uneducated, and unread, without books, without even a newspaper, in a word a mere pretense at a *maskil*. . . .

As I heard later, the *maskil* took me for another *maskil*, and was sure that I should lodge with him, or, at any rate, that he would

be the first one on my list. "For work of that kind," he said to the
others, "you want people with brains. What do you suppose he
could do with the likes of *you*?"

And since the mountain did not go to Mohammed, because he
had never heard of him, Mohammed went to the mountain. He
found me in the house of a widow. He came in with the wicked
child's question in the Haggadah: "What is all this to you?"

"*Moi panyiye!* What are you doing here?"

"How here?" I ask.

"Very likely you think I come from under the stove? That
because a person lives in Tishevitz he isn't civilized, and doesn't
know what is doing in the world? You remember: 'I have so-
journed with Laban'? I do live here, but when there's a rat about I
soon smell him out."

"If you can smell a rat, and know everything that's going on,
why ask questions?"

The beadle pricked up his ears, and so did the half-dozen
loungers who had dogged my steps. There was a fierce delight in
their faces, and on their foreheads was written the verse: "Let the
young men arise"—let us see two *maskilim* have it out between
them!

"What's the good of all this joking?" said the *maskil*, irritated.
"My tongue is not a shoe sole! And for whose benefit am I to
speak? That of the Tishevitz donkeys? Look at the miserable
creatures!"

I feel a certain embarrassment. I cannot very well spring to the
defense of Tishevitz, because the Tishevitz worthies in the window and the doorway are smiling quite pleasantly.

"Come, tell me, what does it all mean, taking notes?"

"Statistics!"

"Statistic-shmistik! We've heard that before. What's the use
of it?"

I explained—not exactly to him, but to the community, so that
they should all have an idea of what statistics meant.

"Ha-ha-ha!" laughs the *maskil* loudly and hoarsely. "You can
get the Tishevitz donkeys to believe that, but not me! Why do you
want to put down how a person lives, with a floor, without a
floor! What does it matter to you if a person lives in a room
without a floor? Ha?"

It matters, I tell him, because people want to show how poor
the Jews are; they think——

"They think nothing of the kind," he interrupted. "But let that pass! Why should they want to know exactly how many boys and how many girls a man has? And what their ages are, and all the rest of the bother?"

"They suspect us of shirking military duty. The records, as of course you know, are not correct, and we want to prove——"

"Well, that may be so, for one thing—I'll allow that—but —about licenses! Why do you note down who has them—and what they are worth?"

"In order to prove that the Jews——"

But the *maskil* won't let me finish my sentence.

"A likely story! Meantime people will know that this one and the other pays less than he ought to for his license, and he'll never hear the last of it."

Hardly had he said this when the heads in the window disappeared; the beadle in the doorway took himself off, and the *maskil*, who had really meant well all along, stood like one turned to stone.

The population had taken fright, and in another hour or two the town was full of talk of me.

I was suspected of being an agent of the excise. And why not, indeed? The excise knew very well that a Jew would have less difficulty in getting behind other people's secrets.

I was left to pace the market square alone. . . .

I arrived in Lyashtzof on a dark summer night, between eleven and twelve o'clock. Another marketplace, with different kinds of buildings and little walled-in houses round about.

In the middle of the marketplace, a collection of large, white stones. I drive nearer—the stones move and sprout horns, they become a herd of milk-white goats.

The goats show more sense than the community leaders of Tishevitz; they are not frightened. One or two of the whole lot lift their heads, look at us sleepily, and once more turn their attention to the scanty grass, and to scratching one another.

Happy goats! No one slanders you, *you* needn't be afraid of statisticians. It is true, people kill you, but what of that? Doesn't everyone die before his time? And as far as troubles go, you certainly have fewer. . . .

Early in the morning, before the arrival of the beadle, there come some Jews—they want to see the note taker. My fame has preceded me.

I make a beginning, and turn to one of them: "Good morning, friend!"

"Good morning, *sholom aleykhem*." He gives me his hand, quite lazily.

"What is your name, friend?"

"Levi-Yitzkhok."

"And your German [family] name?"

"Why do you want to know?"

"Well, is it a secret?"

"Secret or no secret, you may as well tell me why you want to know. I'll be bound *that's* no secret!"

"Then you don't know your German name?"

"Not exactly."

"Make a stab at it—just for fun!"

"Baerenpelz," he answers, a little ashamed.

"A wife?"

"*Ett!*"

"What does *ett* mean?"

"He wants a divorce!" another answers for him.

"How many children?"

He has to think, and counts on his fingers. "By the first wife—mine: one, two, three; hers: one, two. By the second wife . . .

He gets tired of counting: "Let's say six!"

" 'Let's say' is no good. I must know exactly."

"You see, 'exactly' is not so easy. 'Exactly!' Why do you want to know? Are you an official? Do they pay you for it? Will somebody follow and check your statements? 'Exactly!' "

"Tell him, blockhead, tell him," the rest encourage him. "Now you've begun, tell him!" They want to know what the next questions will be.

Once again he has counted on his fingers and, heaven be praised, there are three more. "Nine children, health and strength to them!"

"How many sons, how many daughters?"

He counts again: "Four sons and five daughters."

"How many sons and how many daughters married?"

"You want to know that, too? Look here, tell me why?"

"Tell him, then, tell him!" cry the rest, impatiently.

"Three daughters and two sons," answers someone for him.

"Really?" says the latter. "And Yisrolek?"

"But he isn't married yet."

"Horse! They call him up next Sabbath. What does a week and a half matter?"

I make a note and go on. "Have you served in the army?"

"I bought exemption from *Kahal* [local Jewish authorities], for four hundred rubles! Where should I find them now?" and he groans.

"And your sons?"

"The eldest has a swelling under his right eye, and besides —not of you be it said!—a rupture. He has been in three hospitals. It cost more than a wedding. They only just sent him home from the regiment! The second drew a high number. The third is serving his time now."

"And the wife?"

"At home with me, of course. Why ask?"

"She might have been at *her* father's."

"A pauper!"

"Have you a house?"

"Have I a house!"

"Worth how much?"

"If it were in Zamosc, it would be worth something. Here it's not worth a *drayer*, except that I have a place to lay my head down in."

"Would you sell it for one hundred rubles?"

"The Lord help us! One's own inheritance! Not for three hundred."

"Would you sell it for five hundred?"

"*Meh!* I'd rent a place and go into business!"

"And what is your business now?"

"What business?"

"What do you live on?"

"*That's* what you mean! One just lives."

"On what?"

"God's providence. When He gives something one has it!"

"But He doesn't throw things down from heaven?"

"He does so! Can I tell how I live? Let's figure it out: I need a lot of money, at least four rubles a week. The house brings in, beside my own lodging, twelve rubles a year—nine go for taxes, five for repairs, leaving a hole in the pocket of two rubles a year! That's it."

He puts on airs. "Heaven be praised! I have no money. Neither I, nor any one of the Jews standing here, nor any other

Jews—except perhaps the 'German' ones in the big towns. *We* have no money. I don't know any trade, my grandfather never sewed a shoe. So I live as God wills, and have lived so for fifty years. And if there is a child to be married we have a wedding and dance in the mud."

"Once and for all, what are you?"

"A Jew."

"What do you do all day?"

"I study, I pray—what else should a Jew do? And when I have eaten I go to the market."

"What do you do in the market?"

"What do I do? Whatever turns up. Well, yesterday, for example, I heard, as I passed, that Yoneh Borik wanted to buy three rams for a gentleman. Before daylight I was at the house of a second gentleman who had once said he had too many rams. I made an agreement with Yoneh Borik, and, heaven be praised, we made a ruble and a half by it."

"Are you then what is called a commission agent?"

"How should I know? Sometimes it even occurs to me to buy a bit of produce."

"Sometimes?"

"What do you mean by 'sometimes?' When I have a ruble I buy."

"And when not?"

"I get one."

"How?"

"What do you mean by 'how?' "

And it is an hour before I find out that Levi-Yitzkhok Baeren-pelz is a bit of a rabbinical assistant, and acts as arbiter in quarrels; a bit of a commission agent, a fragment of a merchant, a morsel of a matchmaker, and now and again, when the fancy takes him, a messenger.

Thanks to all these "trades," the counted and the forgotten ones, he earns his bread, though with toil and trouble, for wife and child—even for the married daughter, because her father-in-law is *only* a pauper.

Glossary

ethrog: the fruit of the citron tree, used in the ritual of Sukkoth
gabbai: a deacon
Gemara: a section of the Talmud that interprets the Mishnah
hallah: a twisted white bread used for the Sabbath
Hasidism: a religious movement, based on pietism and enthusiasm,
    which swept through East European Jewry in the eighteenth and
    nineteenth centuries
heder: a Jewish elementary school
Kaddish: mourner's prayer for a deceased close relative, usually said by
    the son
Kiddush: blessing said over a cup of wine to celebrate Sabbath or holiday
kittl: a long robe or coat worn by religious Jews in synagogue
Litvak: a Lithuanian; Lithuania was the center of the traditionalist, con-
    servative, anti-hasidic party
mazel tov: a traditional salutation of congratulations
minyan: a quorum of ten males required for communal religious services
misnagid: an opponent of Hasidism
Mishnah: the oral law which is the basis of the Talmud
mitzvah: a good deed
Reb: a title of respect, roughly equivalent to "Mister" but used with first
    name
rebbe: a hasidic rabbi or leader
rov: rabbi
Seder: the ritual meal celebrating the Passover
shammes: sexton
Shema Yisrael: literally, "Hear, O Israel"; the Jewish credo
Simhath Torah: Feast of the Rejoicing of the Law
shofar: ram's horn blown on High Holidays
shokhet: ritual slaughterer
Sholom aleykhem: the traditional Yiddish greeting; literally, "Peace to
    you"

shtrayml: a round fur hat otten worn by religious Jews
sukkah: a wooden hut with thatched roof used for observance of Sukkoth
Sukkoth: Feast of Booths, the fall harvest festival
tallith: prayer shawl
tzaddik: a hasidic master; a wise or holy man
yarmulke: skullcap worn by religious Jews
Yom Kippur: Day of Atonement, the most sacred day in the Jewish
    religious calendar
Zohar: a kabbalistic book